A FAMILY

UNDER THE
CHRISTMAS TREE

A Novel

TERRI REED

HOWARD BOOKS
An Imprint of Simon & Schuster, Inc.

New York   Nashville   London   Toronto   Sydney   New Delhi

HOWARD BOOKS
An Imprint of Simon & Schuster, Inc.
1230 Avenue of the Americas
New York, NY 10020

First Howard Books trade paperback edition October 2016

HOWARD and colophon are trademarks of Simon & Schuster, Inc.

For information about special discounts for bulk purchases, please contact Simon & Schuster Special Sales at 1-866-506-1949 or business@simonandschuster.com.

The Simon & Schuster Speakers Bureau can bring authors to your live event. For more information or to book an event contact the Simon & Schuster Speakers Bureau at 1-866-248-3049 or visit our website at www.simonspeakers.com.

Manufactured in the United States of America

1   3   5   7   9   10   8   6   4   2

Library of Congress Cataloging-in-Publication Data

Names: Reed, Terri, author.
Title: A family under the Christmas tree / Terri Reed.
Description: First Howard Books trade paperback edition. | New York : Howard Books, 2016.
Subjects: LCSH: Christmas stories. | Domestic fiction. | BISAC: FICTION / Christian / Romance. | FICTION / Romance / Contemporary. | GSAFD: Love stories. | Christian fiction.
Classification: LCC PS3618.E43584 F36 2016 | DDC 813/.6—dc23
LC record available at https://lccn.loc.gov/2016014960

ISBN 978-1-5011-4474-5
ISBN 978-1-5011-4477-6 (ebook)

In loving memory of my mother, Dorothy Louise Westfall,
April 1, 1938–October 15, 2015

A FAMILY

UNDER THE
CHRISTMAS TREE

CHAPTER 1

Sophie Griffith brought her rented car to a stop in the driveway of her grandmother's house. The midday gloom of a rainy December tinted the world in shades of gray. She turned off the engine and looked toward the front door, and smiled as she spied Grandma sitting on the porch, wearing a red and white Santa hat. Little tufts of silver hair peeked out from under the hat, and a green fleece blanket was tucked around her. She waved as Sophie climbed out of the car.

A surge of affection hit her, and Sophie waved back. It had been too long since she'd made the time to visit Grandma. She missed this place. She missed Grandma. She was frustrated that it had taken this for her to make the trip.

Then, she blinked with surprise as she realized Grandma had company. There was a man on her porch. Well, there was a man on a ladder in front of her porch. A man with dark hair and long lean legs, wearing jeans and a black weatherproof jacket, clung to a ten-foot-tall ladder, stringing a strand of icicle lights along the eaves. Shouldn't he be tied off with a safety harness or something?

She held her breath, sure any second he'd topple over as he reached for the little hooks attached to the house.

Sophie returned her narrowed gaze to Grams. Hmmm. Two days ago Grandma had called saying she'd fallen and needed Sophie's help. But she seemed okay now. What was up?

Movement on the lawn drew Sophie's attention. A small boy of about five wearing a blinding yellow beanie streaked across the fenced-in front yard. A muddy dog chased him, close on his heels. Wait, were those reindeer antlers on the dog's head?

The child's sweater could compete in any ugly Christmas sweater contest. His jeans and rain boots were caked in mud. Who was this kid?

The scene reminded her of something from a Hallmark Christmas card. The handsome man, the child and dog playing, Gram supervising it all. . . . She ached to grab her camera and capture the image, but her equipment was out of reach inside hard-sided cases in the back of the SUV.

Sophie grabbed her purse and closed the car door, breathing in the fresh air scented with an earthy musk from a recent rainfall. The cool, damp air seeped through her pink cashmere sweater, but she didn't mind. Hard to believe twenty-four hours and two flight layovers ago she had been baking in the tropical sun. She'd just wrapped up a job photographing the spectacular wedding of one of the year's hottest actors and his makeup artist bride on the island of Gran Canaria, one of the smaller and most popular of the Canary Islands. The average temperature peaked at ninety degrees with high humidity there this time of year. As usual, Grandma's timing was impeccable. Had she called a week earlier, Sophie wouldn't have been available to make the trek to Bellevue, Washington.

Sophie grabbed her suitcases from the trunk. As she tugged the cases up the drive toward the walkway to the house, the man climbed down from the ladder and rushed over.

"Here, let me take those." His voice was rich and deep, and she was surprised to find her stomach flip at the sound.

Not one to turn down help, especially from a handsome man, Sophie relinquished her hold on the bags. "Thank you."

She tilted her head up to meet steel gray eyes fringed with dark lashes. Okay, now that she was seeing him up close, handsome didn't quite cover it. He wasn't beautiful like the Hollywood types she frequently photographed. Some of those guys were prettier than their costars. This man had a square jaw shadowed by day-old scruff and a mouth that tipped upward at the corners in a faint smile.

No, this man's face wasn't pretty, but it had character and strength. And if she wasn't mistaken, there was a hint of melancholy, balanced by an appreciative gleam in his eyes. Her pulse ticked up a notch. She envisioned him within the frame of her lens. The camera would love him. "Nice job with the lights." She tried to make her voice sound natural.

He grinned. "Thank you. My first time."

She blinked. "First time?"

"Putting up Christmas lights."

That explained the lack of safety equipment. "Did Grandma know that when she hired you?"

He laughed, a deep, delicious rumble that Sophie felt in her chest. "We live next door. Louise has been so good to us I offered to put them up."

Ah. A family man. No doubt his wife would be as beautiful as he was.

Now, why did she feel a prick of disappointment at the thought? It was silly. *Get a grip, Soph*, she silently chided herself. The last thing she needed in her life right now was a man. And definitely not a married one.

Sophie had big plans, goals to fulfill. A pending job that she'd been after for a long time. She almost couldn't believe it was really going to happen after all this time. She was not about to get side-tracked. Besides, she didn't do well in the romance department.

The man easily carried the bags to the front porch and set them by the front door. She liked the way he moved, with athletic grace. He was nearly as tall as the doorframe. Not that she should be noticing that kind of thing. She hurried up the porch stairs to her grandmother's side.

"Sophie, my dear, it's so good to see you," Grandma said, her arms spread wide. Her beautiful face beamed. Even at seventy, Grandma hadn't lost her glamour or the twinkle in her blue eyes. Sophie moved into her embrace, relishing the comfort a hug from Grandma could still bring.

Growing up, Sophie had found refuge from her parents' chaotic life at her grandparents' house. Here, Sophie was seen and heard. Here, she wasn't a nuisance. This was the only place Sophie had ever felt like she really belonged.

Sophie owed her grandmother so much. She'd been the one to give Sophie her first camera, when she was twelve. Grandma had seen how hurt she'd been when her older brothers had ditched her to go off on an adventure, as they often did, and Grandma had thought she might enjoy having adventures of her own taking pictures. At the time, she'd had no idea how that one gesture would shape Sophie's future.

Sophie pulled back to look into her grandmother's face, searching for signs of pain. Then she realized Grams wasn't sitting in a normal chair, but an electric wheelchair. "You said you'd fallen. Are you okay?"

Grandma grimaced and moved the blanket covering her legs to reveal a black ankle brace on her right foot. "Sprained it good."

Her stomach clenched. At least it wasn't broken. "What happened?"

Grandma fussed with the blanket. "Oh, well, that's a long story, and one we'll discuss later." She patted her arm. "Where are my manners? Sophie, dear, this is my new neighbor, David Murphy."

David tugged off his glove and held out his hand. "Hello, Sophie."

She slipped her hand into his, and his big hand engulfed hers. Their palms fit together, and his fingers curled over hers firmly. "It's nice to meet you, David. Thank you for getting the lights up for my grandmother."

His gaze never left her face. Nor did he retract his hand. "You're welcome. Louise has told me a great deal about you."

"All good, I hope." Sophie slid a glance to Grandma, who winked. Sophie did a double take. Grandma's smile was pure innocence.

Sophie's gaze narrowed. She hadn't imagined the wink. What was Grandma doing? The man was taken. Maybe Grandma's mind was impaired along with her foot.

David chuckled. "Yes, all good. She's very proud of you and your talent."

Touched by his words, Sophie smiled. "Well, she's the one who sparked my interest in photography."

"I'd like to see your work sometime."

An image of them sitting cozily in front of a roaring fire, clicking through the pages of her portfolios, flashed into her mind. Her cheeks heated. There was no reason why what he'd said should sound so intimate. Maybe it was the way he held her gaze or the interest flaring in the depths of his stormy eyes.

Stop it, she told herself. Stop it now.

Heat continued to bloom in her cheeks and she realized she was still holding his hand. He followed her gaze to their joined palms. He took in a sharp gasp of air and quickly slipped his hand away, then shoved both of his hands into the pockets of his jacket and stepped back.

"Troy!" David called to the boy on the lawn.

David's son pounded up the stairs and came to a skidding halt next to him. The dog, which on closer inspection was a large black, brown, and white puppy, bounded up the steps and nudged himself between David's legs. The antlers snagged on David's knee and slid sideways. She wished once again she'd had her camera ready.

Sophie had to force herself not to tell them to freeze while she went to grab it. She needed to keep it close if she wanted to catch opportunities like this one.

"Riggs." Grandmother snapped her fingers to get the puppy's attention and then motioned the dog to her side.

Sophie stared as the dog obeyed and moved to sit beside Grandma's chair.

David put his hand on his son's shoulder. "This is Troy."

Sophie shifted her attention to the child and smiled. "Hello, Troy. I'm Sophie."

The kid stuck out his hand and gave her hand a quick shake. "Nice to meet ya. You're pretty just like Grandma Louise said."

Sophie arched an eyebrow at her grandmother. Grandma smiled serenely, as if telling strangers she had a pretty grand-daughter was the most natural thing in the world. Turning back to Troy, Sophie asked, "How old are you, Troy?"

He puffed up his chest. "I'm five. I'm in kindergarten."

"Nice." She lifted her gaze to find David watching her.

"We've got to get going." David tugged at the collar of his coat. "I've work to do."

"Awww, Uncle David, not yet," Troy said, looking up at David. "Me and Riggs are having a good time."

So. Not father and son, as she'd assumed. Her pulse skipped a beat. She glanced at David's ring finger. No shiny band.

Uh-oh. Now Grandma's wink made sense. Sophie wouldn't put it past her grandmother to try setting Sophie up for a holiday romance. Not going to happen.

Sophie liked her nomadic lifestyle, roaming wherever the jobs took her. She had no inclination to make a change now. Or anytime in the future. She'd imagined she'd found The One more than once and the relationship had failed each time. Miserably. Much to her mother's chagrin.

Better to not try again than find herself with another broken heart.

But even if David was off-limits, she was curious about Troy.

Was the boy visiting his uncle? Had the child's parents dropped him off, too busy with their own lives to care for their son?

Old resentments sparked deep inside Sophie and she quickly quashed them. Not all parents chose their careers over their children. Hadn't her therapist warned her often enough not to project her past onto others?

David's jaw tightened and his voice was measured when he answered. "I understand. But it's time to go home."

"I don't want to go!" Troy stamped a foot.

Sophie pressed her lips together and waited to see how David would react.

David leveled a stern look on the child. "Troy, remember our deal."

Troy's expression turned mutinous as he held his uncle's gaze in a classic power play. She'd seen her brothers do it with their father numerous times over the years.

Neither flinched. Then Troy's tiny shoulders sagged. "Yeah. I can play in the mud with Riggs as long as I don't make a fuss when it's time to go home." Troy blew out a frustrated little breath. "Okay." He turned and hugged Grandma. "'Bye, Grandma Louise."

Sophie's heart melted a little at how sweet the child was to her grandmother. Troy met Sophie's gaze. "'Bye, Sophie."

"Good-bye, Troy. It was nice to meet you."

He smiled and gave Riggs a hug before thumping down the stairs and across the driveway toward the house next door. The beige and dark brown exterior of the charming single-story home blended well with the older residences on the street. Brick accents along the foundation added an interesting visual touch, and the evergreen bushes and trees in the yard were well groomed.

David sighed and watched him go. "Does it ever get easier?" he asked Louise.

"It will, David. Be patient." Grandmother adjusted the blanket on her lap. "He's a great kid. He just needs some time to adjust."

Sophie felt awkward standing there listening in as this man sought advice from her grandmother. She shifted and stepped back a bit.

David nodded and flashed a quick glance at Sophie. "Goodbye. I hope you enjoy your stay." He turned back to Louise and smiled. "Thank you for your help." He hurried after Troy.

Sophie watched the two disappear through a hole in the row of hedges that separated Grandmother's house from the newer one next door. At one time, Grandma and Grandpa had owned the adjacent lot. Back then it had been a wooded wonderland, the perfect place for Sophie and her brothers to play when they came to visit. She cried her eyes out the day the trees had been cut down and dragged away.

Sophie heard a door close. "Where are Troy's parents?"

Grandma hesitated a moment before she spoke. "There was a car accident this past summer," she finally replied. "Both parents were killed."

Sophie's heart twisted. So that explained the melancholy she'd noticed in both David and Troy. "That's so sad."

"Yes, it is."

Sophie waited for her to go on, but she didn't say anything more.

Something wet nudged Sophie's hand. She glanced down to see the puppy staring up at her with big brown eyes. He was still wearing the crooked antler. She squatted down and dug her fingers into his soft fur. There was something so soothing about petting the pup.

"Oh, my. He's so cute." She looked at Grams. "Riggs, uh? That's an interesting name. What kind of dog is he?"

"Bernese mountain dog," Grandma said. "He's ten months old and already so big."

Riggs licked Sophie's face. She laughed and wiped off a glob of slobber. "Who does he belong to?"

When Grandma didn't answer, Sophie's gaze shot back to Grandma. There was a gleam in her blue eyes.

"Grams?"

Grandma sighed. "He's mine. But I was hoping that maybe you'd like to have him."

Sophie jerked upright. "Uh, that would be a no. Grams, I can't take on a dog. I'm never in one place long enough to care for an animal. Let alone a big one like this guy."

Riggs leaned into her legs and licked her hand. Sophie stepped away. He was cute, but there was no way she was going to let the puppy worm his way into her heart. "Why did you get a dog, anyway?"

Grandma plucked at the fuzz on the blanket. "I was lonely. And Simon suggested I get a pet. A cat might have been a better choice, but I saw Riggs at the Humane Society and fell in love with him."

Sophie's heart clutched. Of course Grandma was lonely living here alone. She should have thought about that. The rest of the family lived in Southern California, and Grandpa had passed over a decade ago. Guilt slithered through Sophie. She should have made more of an effort to visit more frequently. She'd have to tell her brothers they also needed to make the effort to come see Grandma.

But one thing Grandma had said confused her.

"Who's Simon?"

Sophie narrowed her gaze. Was that a blush tingeing Grandma's cheeks? Or was it just the cold air giving her a rosy hue? In this light it was hard to tell.

"He's a friend from church," Grandma said. "We serve together on the Helping Hands committee." Grandma fiddled with the controls on her wheelchair. The wheels hummed and spun, and the chair turned so that she now faced the front door. "It's getting chilly out here. Shall we go in?"

Hmmm. Definitely a blush. Interesting. She'd need to find out more about that soon. For now, she hurried to open the door.

"Riggs will need to be wiped down. Do you mind? I'm not sure I could manage it. I can barely get myself bathed and dressed on one good foot," Grandma said as she pushed her chair inside the warm house. "There's a bucket for water and towels in the laundry room."

Sophie eyed Riggs. The white and tan parts of his coat were crusted with mud and they nearly matched the black parts of his fur. His head tilted as he watched her, waiting patiently, as if he'd been trained to anticipate the need for a bath before entering the house. Surely Grandma hadn't summoned her just to care for the dog?

No, Sophie had a strong feeling that Grandma's intentions weren't that pedestrian. Sophie believed that she did need help after her fall, but she was pretty sure that wasn't all she had in mind.

With a little huff, Sophie went to fetch the bucket and towels.

❄   ❄   ❄

The stunning Sophie Griffith was one more distraction David didn't need. He stared at the charcoal etching with frustration. Louise had mentioned on more than a few occasions that her unmarried granddaughter was coming to visit.

He had the distinct impression Louise was hoping something might kindle between him and Sophie. He suspected that was why she'd asked if he'd put up her lights yesterday at the exact time Sophie was to arrive.

He'd been amused by her meddling until he saw the leggy blonde step out of her car and he'd felt a visceral reaction in his gut. She was tall, which he liked, and her clear blue eyes had missed nothing. She seemed to stare at everything at once and he'd wondered if she was imagining what the world would look like with the perfect lighting and the correct angle for her camera lens.

Louise had said Sophie was pretty, but "pretty" was such a mild word. She wasn't model gorgeous in that surreal way that some women had. No, Sophie's beauty was natural. Her golden skin spoke of other places, warm and sunny places. Her blond hair had hung loose about her shoulders and framed an oval face that he'd itched to draw the second he'd returned to his desk. Now that drawing stared back at him, pulling his mind away from his work.

He pushed the sketchbook aside. He couldn't let anything or anyone divert his attention. Operating a million-dollar company and raising a child—especially one you hadn't planned on—was hard enough. The last thing he needed was to add a complication such as romance into the mix. Romances, he'd found, took energy and effort that he didn't have right now. He'd discovered early on that along with love came heartache. It was a state of being he didn't want to experience ever again.

He refocused on his computer, which he'd set up in the dining room so he could work and keep an eye on Troy. Juggling the sudden demands of single parenthood and the company he'd built from the ground up was taxing not only his energy but also his emotional reserves.

After his brother and sister-in-law's tragic deaths, David had been granted custody of his nephew, a fate David had never expected. Why had Daniel and Beth appointed him guardian of their son?

David and Daniel had had such different lives the past few years. They hadn't seen eye to eye on many things. David had been focused on building his company, Daniel on taking care of his family. Daniel had been clearly disappointed that David had devoted himself to work instead of family and faith. He'd said as much to David on more than one occasion.

Guilt ate at David for allowing a wedge to develop between him and Daniel. A wedge that had been shattered by Daniel's death.

And now, six months into fatherhood, David still felt like he was walking through a minefield. To say it was overwhelming would be an understatement.

There was no class to prepare someone to become a parent overnight. David was not only struggling with his own grief over his brother's passing, but he was trying his best to help Troy cope as well. Some days were better than others.

Yesterday had been good. Troy and Riggs had played hard for a couple of hours, and Troy had been exhausted by the time they'd returned home, which allowed David some focused time at his computer.

David hoped today would be good too, but Troy hadn't slept well. Ever since Daniel and Beth's accident, Troy had been struggling with nightmares—night terrors, the doctor called them—that left him screaming and afraid. The next day, they would both be cranky. But they'd managed to make breakfast together, do their laundry, and make their beds without any meltdowns. He considered that a success.

With school out for the holiday break, Troy was in the living room watching a cartoon. The volume crept up to a deafening level and grated on David's already tightly strung nerves.

He was working to develop a sensor for smartphones that would determine a person's hydration level. The sensor would be able to read the saturation in their skin when a finger was pressed against the sensor, and it would be connected to an app that would track and monitor this.

The idea came after a reporter for a national online newspaper had issued a challenge to software designers to develop a number of seemingly outlandish apps. Every software developer in David's sphere had been abuzz about the list of wished-for apps. Some were too ridiculous to contemplate, while others had merit.

Like an app that detected when someone was dehydrated.

As David had done research into the negative effects of dehydration, he saw how useful such an app could be. He'd begun working on it nearly a year ago, and was now at the final stages. This project could be the one that set his company up for life. So much was riding on getting it right. And rolling the app out before anyone else got wind of it was paramount.

But to succeed, David needed time. Uninterrupted, focused time.

He rose and strode to the archway of the living room. Troy sat on the floor with his legs crisscrossed as a set of animated superheroes saved the world.

"Hey, buddy, can we turn the volume down a couple of clicks?" David asked.

Troy ignored him. David stepped over a dump truck to pick up the remote from the coffee table and decreased the sound. Troy seemed not to notice.

Shaking his head, David returned to his project. His hands flew over the keyboard of his computer. He made notes on a yellow legal pad. He was so close. This app could save lives if he could get it to run correctly.

Ten minutes later, Troy raced into the room and jumped on David's back. The chair squeaked with the extra weight. David took a deep breath and tried to summon as much patience as he could. Then David lifted his hands from his keyboard and took a deep breath. "Troy. I'm working."

"You promised we could go to the park!" Troy jumped down and twirled in a circle. "I want to go to the park."

"You're right. I did say we'd go to the park. Later. But I need to work now."

"All you do is work," Troy said, his face set in a mulish look. This didn't bode well. "I want to play."

"Troy, we'll go to the park after lunch."

"No! I want to go *now!*" he shouted.

Cringing from the high decibel noise coming from the small child, David grit his teeth. "Do not yell at me." He tried to keep his voice even and calm, like the books had told him to.

"You promised," Troy said in the same tone of voice.

Again, David took a deep breath and answered calmly. "Do not raise your voice at me." His hands gripped the chair, and he noticed that his knuckles were turning white. "We will go to the park when I am done here."

"Well, I'm going to go now," Troy said. His voice was quieter, but laced with challenge.

"You are not going to go to the park on your own. We will—"

"You can't tell me what to do!" Troy screeched. "You're not my daddy!"

David's heart sank. The accusation shredded his insides. He'd been warned that Troy would act out in his grief. David was barely processing his own sorrow at the loss of his brother; he couldn't imagine how hard this had to be for Troy.

Patience, he told himself. He knelt down and gripped Troy's slender shoulders. Looking into his face, David saw his brother in the jut of Troy's chin, in the shape of his eyes. Sadness swamped him, making his eyes burn. "I know I'm not your father. I can't replace Daniel. But, Troy, you and I are all either of us has in this world. We have to figure out how to live together."

"I don't want to live with you anymore." Troy wrenched free, and he ran toward the front door.

"Troy, no!" David raced after his nephew. David's feet tangled in the Thomas the Tank engine tracks that lay in the middle of the living room, and he fell to his knees as Troy ran out of the house into the wet, cold, rainy day. Without a hat or coat.

Pure panic gripped David. All sorts of horrible scenarios played through his head. "Oh, Dear Father in Heaven, please don't let anything happen to him." The prayer slipped out, surprising him. He wasn't really sure where he stood with God, but he'd been raised to believe. Apparently in a crisis, default mode was to turn to Him.

He jumped to his feet, grabbed his and Troy's jackets, and chased after his nephew.

CHAPTER 2

Sophie clicked a leash to Riggs's collar. She was dressed for the rain with mud boots, waterproof pants, and a raincoat over a warm sweater. She knew better than to come to the Pacific Northwest in December unprepared. "Come on, dog. We're going to let Grandma rest."

Grandma had settled in a recliner by the fire, her feet up and a blanket covering her. A book lay open in her lap but her eyes were closed. Sophie smiled with tender affection.

After a filling breakfast and some Christmas planning—decorating the house, shopping online for the family, and recipes to make for their holiday dinner—Grandma had taken to her chair while Sophie finished unpacking her things into the guest room. Not much had changed in the house since her childhood. The same green comforter covered the trundle bed. The same lace curtains, yellowed with age, hung over the window that looked out on the small backyard.

The hallway was lined with framed photographs, starting with black-and-white images of her grandparents from back when they were first married and moving through time with each subsequent picture. It was like watching her family's lives unfold.

Sophie touched the images of her grandfather with fond remembrance. He'd been a big man with a large laugh. If she closed her eyes and listened she could hear the echo of his laughter filling the house.

In the living room, the knickknacks Sophie had played with as a child still sat on the shelves of the hutch in the corner. She'd liked to pretend the blue glass swan was a princess in disguise and the ceramic farm animal figurines were trying to help the princess find her way home.

The mantel clock softly ticked away the time. Warmth from the fire filled the house, and the hint of Grandma's gardenia perfume teased Sophie's nose. The smell brought back memories of curling up under the orange afghan on the couch and watching old movies with her grandparents.

She was amazed by how happy she was to be here, to be back to the one place she'd always felt at home. And she was surprised by how much she was looking forward to spending Christmas here. She couldn't wait to get a Christmas tree and dig out the box of old ornaments that Grandma had said was packed away in the attic. They also planned to do some serious baking, something Sophie hadn't had time for in ages—let alone a place. She tended to spend most of her days and nights in hotel rooms on assignments that took her around the globe. Her small studio apartment in Burbank was more of a landing pad and staging area than an actual living space.

Riggs was pulling on the leash, so Sophie cast one more glance back at Grandma and saw that she was sleeping. Then she followed behind as Riggs tugged the leash all the way toward the door. Sophie figured a little exercise and fresh air would do her and the dog good. Though Riggs wouldn't be getting the same type of workout he'd had yesterday with the neighbor's nephew. What a cute kid!

And his uncle was pretty cute, too. Tall, broad-shouldered, and dark-haired. The stuff of girlhood dreams. Okay, maybe some adult dreams, too. She couldn't stop thinking about the flare of interest she'd seen in his eyes or the stirring of attraction she'd felt.

Not that it meant anything.

She probably wouldn't even see David again while she was here. Well, maybe in passing. A friendly wave. A Christmas greeting. Nothing more.

Getting involved was not on her agenda. Her focus while in Washington was to get Grandma back on both feet. Then Sophie would be off on another job. Hopefully with a prestigious skiwear company, though she didn't want to get her hopes up. She'd had that particular dream quashed before.

But that was then. This time the company had come to her. Or rather her agent. She'd been pursuing jobs with them for a long time, and it looked like her career was finally starting to take. She wanted to be one of the top commercial photographers in the country, and she had worked very hard to get there.

And she'd learned from painful experience that pursuing her dream didn't line up well with romantic relationships. Boyfriends tended not to like it when she was gone for weeks at a time. They got insecure when she was photographing some of the best-looking men in the world. They didn't understand that just because she was traveling to exotic places, she was not on vacation. Better, she had discovered, to stay focused on what she could control. Men certainly were not on that list.

Riggs's nails clicked on the hardwood floor as he danced with excitement at the prospect of going out for a walk. His long, bushy tail swept from side to side. He really was a handsome pup, all fluffy and very masculine. One could never mistake Riggs for a girl dog. His striking coloring and expressive face would photograph well.

Which reminded her . . .

"Stay put," she said, and dashed back to her room to grab her camera from its case. She put a bright blue rain cover over the equipment for protection from the rain and then slipped the camera strap over her head and rested the camera against her chest.

After grabbing the ball thrower from the laundry room, Sophie tugged her rainhat over her ears, buttoned her coat, and opened the front door. A blast of cold rain greeted her. For half a second she contemplated aborting the idea of a walk, but Riggs rushed out the door, pulling her along with him. She held tight to the end of the leash as she shut the door behind her.

The dog stopped at the top of the steps to glance back at her as if to say *hurry up*. She tucked the ball thrower under her arm and snapped off a few shots of him with her camera. Was he smiling?

With a rueful laugh, she let Riggs take the lead and hurried to keep up.

"Do you know where you're going?" she asked him. He did seem to know the way to the wooded community park that she'd intended to take him to. The park had tennis courts, basketball hoops, a playground, and a dog off-leash area. They didn't encounter anyone as they walked through the neighborhood, but she was struck with a sense of nostalgia.

How many times had she and her brothers made this trek to the playground? Back then her grandparents had never been far behind, always wanting to keep a watchful eye on their grandchildren.

There'd been other kids in the neighborhood who'd sometimes come out to play with the Griffith kids when they visited. Sophie wondered whatever happened to Amy Keen, a girl the same age as Sophie. Amy had had dark hair and a bright smile. They'd become fast friends and had promised to be friends forever. They'd stayed in touch until middle school.

Then Amy's letters had dried up and Sophie's cards had been returned stamped NO LONGER AT THIS ADDRESS. Grandma had said Mr. Keen had been transferred to a job overseas. The loss of Amy's friendship had stung.

Sophie and Riggs reached the park and entered the fenced-in, off-leash dog area. As Riggs sniffed around, Sophie stared across the street at the blue house on the corner that had once belonged to the Keens. Someone had hung lights and set up an inflatable snowman in the front yard.

The echo of a yearning she hadn't felt in a very long time throbbed in her chest. She'd enjoyed spending time with the Keens. They'd been a kind and loving family who had actually eaten dinner together.

That was unheard of in Sophie's life. Both of her parents had very demanding Hollywood careers that required long hours away from home. A string of nannies had attempted to fill the void over the years, but Sophie had always felt the lack of connection to her parents. Still did, if truth were told. Even though her parents had recently slowed down, they were strangers to her in many ways.

Riggs let out a short bark. He sat on his haunches and cocked his head at her, his eyes locked on the ball thrower. He was clearly waiting for her to pay attention to him.

She laughed and unleashed him. "Okay, you. We'll play until I'm too cold to throw the ball anymore."

Thankfully, the rain had subsided to a misty drizzle. She threw the ball, and then quickly brought her camera up to capture action shots of Riggs as he whipped around and raced through the mud after the flying tennis ball. His paws flung mud and water everywhere.

Her heart beat with excitement. She knew she'd gotten some great shots that she could add to her portfolio. Riggs found the ball where it landed, and he loped back to her side to drop it at her feet. All the while she kept clicking away.

"Hmmm. Someone has trained you well." She picked up the slobbery ball. "Ick." She popped it back into the thrower and then wiped her hand on her coat. "Don't get used to this, dog. We're going to have to find you a new home after Christmas. Grandma can't take care of you. You are too big, too much."

Riggs shuffled closer and licked her hand, then stared up at her with soulful brown eyes that seemed to plead with her to love him. Tender affection budded within her and she took several pictures of him. She came out from behind the lens to say, "Stop looking at me like that."

She threw the ball again and marveled at Riggs's agility as he chased after it.

She'd have to make sure to find him a good home. Someplace that would be able to accommodate a dog of his size. He already was past her knee and would only grow bigger when he matured.

Riggs scampered toward her, carrying the ball in his mouth, and then skidded to a stop a few feet away. His ears perked up. His nose lifted. He dropped the ball and let out a bark. She captured the change in him with her camera.

"What are you doing?" she asked him.

Riggs shifted to face her, barked again, and then ran to the gate. Her mouth dropped open. She kept taking pictures as he jumped up. His huge paw hit the release mechanism on the gate, allowing the gate door to swing open.

He raced through the opening like his feet were on fire. She sputtered with astonishment and took off after him. What if he darted into the street and was hit by a car?

Dread spread through her like a virus, making her stomach roil with nausea. She couldn't let anything happen to him. "Riggs, come back!"

The dog ignored her and darted around the brick building that housed the restrooms.

"Riggs!" Her sneakers slipped and slid on the slick grass. She tucked her camera to the side so that her arm could hold it like a football and it wouldn't be damaged bouncing against her ribs. Mud and water soaked her jeans as she ran in an effort to keep up with the much faster Riggs.

She rounded the edge of the restrooms in time to see the dog disappear into the thick shadows of the woods that bordered the park. Oh, no. She'd never catch him. But she had to try.

She ran harder and caught sight of a dark figure in her peripheral vision a second before they collided.

David.

His identity registered in the split second before her feet slipped out from beneath her.

Her arms cartwheeled. The camera bounced against her ribs. The world tilted. She brought her elbows in and curled around the camera protectively, bracing herself for a fall.

But strong arms snaked around her, catching her and drawing her close. Her nose was buried in the wet folds of his weatherproof jacket. Her feet dangled in the air for a moment before he set her down.

"Whoa. Are you okay?" he asked.

She gripped the lapels of his coat and leaned back to look up into his anxious face. "Yes. Sorry. I didn't mean to slam into you."

"No, my bad. I didn't see you until the last second." He stepped back. He held a child's rain slicker in his hands. Worry darkened his eyes. "Have you seen Troy?"

Concern flooded her. "No. What happened?"

David threaded the fingers of his free hand through his dark, wet hair. "We had an argument and he ran out the door. I was hoping to find him at the playground but he's not there."

Sophie looked around, as if he might be nearby. "I haven't seen him," she said.

David pinched the bridge of his nose. "I can't believe I let this happen."

"Hey now. He's a kid. It's not your fault."

But David just shook his head. "I'm horrible at this parent thing. They should never have picked me to be Troy's guardian." He drew in a deep breath, trying to pull himself together. "I have to find him."

Filled with anxiety, Sophie offered, "I'll help you search."

"I'd appreciate it, thanks." David pointed to the women's restroom. "Can you check in there? I'll get the men's room."

Riggs reappeared from the tree line, drawing their attention with a series of barks. Then he whirled away to once again disappear into the trees. Crazy dog.

"What's he doing?" David asked as he moved toward the men's restroom.

"I have no clue. He let himself out of the dog park and ran

into the trees," she explained. She hurried to the women's restroom and checked the stalls. Empty.

She met David in front of the building. She shook her head to let him know she hadn't found Troy.

"Where could he have gone?" David pulled out his cell phone. "I have to call the police."

Riggs returned to the same spot and barked again. This time the pitch intensified, became more insistent.

"Riggs, come," Sophie called, a good dose of frustration lacing her tone.

The dog dashed forward and then backed up, all the while barking frantically.

"I think he's trying to get us to follow him," David said. "Maybe he found Troy." He rushed to trail after the dog.

"Now, that would be a Christmas miracle." Sophie hurried to catch up to David. *Please, Lord, let us find Troy safe and sound.*

Riggs's barking led them through the trees to the far corner of the park. The dog paced in front of a large evergreen bush until he noticed them. He raced over to them.

Sophie made a grab for Riggs's collar. The dog dodged her attempt to control him and ran back to the bush. He pawed at the ground, sticking his nose into the branches, and then gave her a look that made her feel like she was missing something.

Sophie met David's confused and worried gaze. "Troy?"

"Troy!" David called out.

Riggs cocked his head, then lay down to shuffle beneath the bush until all that was visible was his back end. Unable to resist, she brought the camera lens into focus and snapped off several shots.

"Troy must be under there," Sophie whispered to David. Riggs had heard or smelled Troy, or maybe both, and had somehow understood the boy was in trouble and needed help. Smart dog.

David knelt down and army-crawled under the bush next to Riggs. Sophie pressed her lips together to keep a giggle from escaping. The situation wasn't in the least funny. Troy had run away from David and hidden under the bush. He was safe, but he'd scared them something fierce.

But the image of the dog and man buried to the waist beneath the leafy branches was too comical for her not to smile. She took a number of shots. She could hear the velvety tenor of David's voice as he talked with Troy, who refused to come out of his hiding spot.

She approached the space and squatted down beside David. Though she could see only the whites of Troy's eyes in the murky depths of the shrub, she said, "Hey, Troy, if you'll come out, you can help walk Riggs home."

"Really?" His little voice was followed by a hiccup.

"Yes, really."

Soon both Riggs and David wiggled back out from beneath the thick plant, along with Troy. All three were soaked and layered with mud. Through the lens of her camera she captured the expression of relief on David's handsome face. She caught Troy's tear-streaked cheeks and Riggs's proud countenance. These shots would add so much character and life to her portfolio.

David put the coat around Troy's shoulders before lifting the boy into his arms to hug him close. She took another picture, capturing the tender moment.

There was something so precious about the man and boy. A lump formed in Sophie's throat and she quickly leashed Riggs, mostly to give her something to do to cover the emotion that welled up uncontrollably inside her.

"You scared me," David said to Troy.

"Sorry, Uncle David," the boy said, hanging his head. He lifted his deep blue gaze to Sophie. "Can I walk Riggs now?"

Sophie gave David a questioning look, not wanting to usurp his authority with the child. The relief and love on his face softened her heart even more. He nodded and set Troy on his feet.

Sophie held out the loop of the leash. "We'll both hold the loop," she told him. She was afraid the puppy would drag the slight child.

As they walked back through the neighborhood, Sophie and Troy walked ahead of David. She glanced back several times and wondered at his pensive expression. Was he berating himself again? She felt bad for him. He was in a difficult situation, but he was doing the best he could, wasn't he? She respected that he was trying. How many single men in their early thirties would give up their freedom to raise a child alone?

At the walkway to David and Troy's house, David stopped. "Time to let go of the leash, Troy. We're home."

"*Noooo*," Troy protested. "I want to walk Riggs all the way to his house."

David's jaw tightened for a second. He probably had a million things to do. The guy had to have a job of some sort. At the very least, his patience had to be at its limit. But instead of saying no, he sighed. "All right. If Sophie doesn't mind."

"Not at all," she was quick to assure them both. She wasn't sure giving into Troy's demands was the correct path to take, but the pair had been through enough today. No doubt David wanted to avoid another tantrum.

Over Troy's head, David said, "Thank you. You have no idea how much I appreciate your help."

"I didn't do much," she remarked. "Riggs found him. He's a smart dog."

David smiled but she could see the residual fear and exhaustion in his eyes. The incident in the park had taken a toll on him.

"Yes, he is." He held her gaze. She liked the way the gray light filtering through the overcast sky touched the silver threads in his eyes. "Still, I don't know if I'd have been able to get Troy to come out from beneath the bush without chopping the thing down if you hadn't been there. You were amazing."

Warm pleasure shot through her. Crazy how his simple compliment made her feel so special. "You're welcome."

When they reached Grandma's yard, Sophie unhooked the leash from Riggs's collar. The dog let out a happy yelp and raced around the yard, with Troy close on his heels.

She sat on the porch steps to watch them play. David sat next to her. He was a hot mess, covered in mud, with debris clinging to his hair and clothes. But he was still so handsome. She had to resist the urge to wipe away a streak of mud from his chin.

She was cold from the rain, and mud soaked into her jeans and boots. She really should go inside to warm up, but she was content to sit next to David and watch Troy and Riggs play. This was not how she'd expected this day to go at all.

"What do you do?" she finally asked, giving in to her curiosity. "Workwise."

"I'm in I.T."

Information technology. A computer geek. "Does that mean if my computer has a glitch or crashes, you're the guy I call?"

He chuckled. "Something like that."

"Not that I've turned my computer on since I arrived."

"No?"

"Nope. I really only use it to upload my photos or send files. I use my phone for everything else." She took her phone from the pocket of her jacket. The home screen had three notifications. "Ooops. I missed a call from my agent and my dad." Odd. Dad rarely called. She hoped everything was okay. He'd have left a message if there was a problem, right?

"I didn't know photographers had agents."

"Most talent industries do."

"Do you need to call your agent back? Maybe they have a big job for you?"

"She left a voice message and a text message." She swiped the screen and read the text. It asked her to check her email. She opened the email program and found the message from Larissa. She felt a smile creep across her face as she read.

"Good news?"

"Yes. I'm doing a big shoot in January with a national-brand skiwear company." She hugged the phone to her chest. "They're confirming my availability." She shivered with delight.

"Skiwear, huh? Where will they send you?"

"The Alps. All that lovely snow." She giggled. "The best excuse to buy new cold weather clothes."

"Congratulations."

"Let's hope so. Just because they put me on hold, meaning they have first dibs on my time, doesn't mean they will actually use me. It could fall through. But this is still huge. I've been trying to get in with them for years. It's the kind of job every commercial and fashion photographer hopes for. If I get it, it will mean lots more work down the road. Larissa says she'll have firm travel details from them by Christmas."

"When would you leave?"

She glanced at the email details. "I'm guessing right after New Year's. This is perfect timing." Everything was falling into place. She sent up a silent prayer that nothing would derail her plans.

CHAPTER
3

Sitting there on Louise's front porch, wet and cold from chasing Troy, David's mind kept going back to the fear he'd felt when he thought he'd lost the child. To the joy of finding him. To how very grateful he was for Sophie and Riggs.

He slanted an appreciative glance at the woman seated next to him. Her rain hat was askew, and her clothes were wet and splattered with mud. Her cheeks were flushed and her blue eyes were bright like a summer day as she met his gaze.

Daniel would have said that God had sent David his own private miracle in the form of a beautiful woman and an uncannily intelligent dog. David wasn't too sure he trusted God or anyone else to care about him that much. Faith had been Daniel's thing.

David's gaze dropped to Sophie's mouth. Her lush lips curved in a soft smile. The longing to lean close and kiss her gripped him in a tight vise. His mouth went dry and he jerked his gaze away.

Not going there.

He didn't want or need any additional complications in his life. He had more than enough to deal with, and adding an attraction to his neighbor's granddaughter wasn't an option.

"I should take Troy home and get him cleaned up," David said, breaking the silence. He needed some distance.

"Right." She scrambled to her feet. "Me, too. I mean, not the go with you part, but I should get Riggs cleaned up. And myself."

She was cute all flustered. Maybe he wasn't the only one feeling the pull of attraction here. That was a dangerous thought. Yet, his ego didn't mind too much.

The front door opened and Louise rolled out in her wheelchair. "I thought I heard voices out here." She looked David up and down. "Oh, my. Did you fall in a mud puddle?"

He glanced down at himself. His jeans were filthy and stained brown. The front of his jacket was crusted with dirt. He didn't even want to think about the mud in his hair and plastered to his face. He did look like he'd fallen in a mud puddle. Great. He hadn't felt this uncomfortable and self-conscious since high school. Definitely time to go.

"Something like that," he said. "Troy, let's go home."

"Awww, Uncle David! Not yet." Troy doggedly hung on to a tree branch while Riggs held the other end between his teeth and backed up, nearly dragging Troy off balance.

Sensing another scene coming on, David braced himself. "Troy, please."

"Oh, my," Louise said as she caught sight of Troy. She laughed. "It seems you all took a bath in the mud."

"Troy ran away," Sophie said softly, so Troy wouldn't hear. "We found him hiding under a bush in the park. David and Riggs went in after him."

Concern drew Louise's eyebrows together. "Why would he do that?"

"I'd promised him we'd go to the park, but I had work to get done first. He didn't want to wait." David rubbed a hand over his chin. Flakes of dried mud fell away into his palm. He dropped his hand. "I don't know how to make him understand that I have responsibilities to my staff and my company."

"Have you thought about hiring a nanny?" Sophie asked.

"He's in school most of the time, so it's not such an issue. He's off for two weeks for the holidays, and that's what's been difficult."

"But surely you could get someone to help out until he goes back to school."

He hesitated. "The grief counselor I met with advised against bringing a stranger into the house while Troy's still in a fragile stage of the grieving process. But I'll have to hire one come summertime."

"He's welcome to come over here," Louise said. "Sophie and I are going to bake cookies this afternoon. Why don't you take him home, get him bathed, and then bring him back for a couple of hours."

"Grandma, are you sure you're up to it?" Sophie's voice hitched up an octave. Clearly she didn't think it was a good idea.

"Sophie, dear, David needs some help." She smiled. "Besides, it will be fun."

David could see Sophie's reluctance and really wanted to let her off the hook. He owed her big time already for coaxing Troy out from beneath the bush. Letting Troy walk Riggs was an inspired idea. How had she known that would be the right thing to make him want to come out of his hiding spot?

An anxious little quiver struck a chord within his chest. He didn't like owing anyone anything. He prided himself on his ability to accomplish what he had in life without the help of anyone he didn't employ.

Growing up poor had instilled in him the need for financial security and independence. It was a feat he was close to achieving. He'd had his fill of charity. Been there, done that. He didn't want to be on the receiving end of "good works" ever again.

A little whisper of doubt snaked through him. He knew nothing in life was guaranteed. Certainly not with today's economy. But he'd followed all the steps, taken all the precautions he could to secure his future. His gaze strayed to where Troy and Riggs continued to play tug-of-war with a branch.

It was a future that now included Troy.

But that future would be in jeopardy if David didn't get back to work.

Still, imposing any more on Sophie and Louise rankled. "That's okay. We'll manage."

"Nonsense." Louise leveled a determined look at him.

He drew in his chin. He made a mental note not to get on her bad side.

"You bring him over for some cookie baking." Louise took Sophie's hand. "We insist."

He met Sophie's troubled gaze. "I don't want to intrude on your time with your grandma."

The hesitation in her eyes cleared and her expression softened. "He's more than welcome to join us."

Relief eased the tension in his shoulders. "Thank you. We'll be back in a little bit." He hurried down the stairs and across the yard. Troy saw him coming and began shaking his head. "Sophie and Louise have invited you to help them make Christmas cookies. Would you like that?"

A grin broke out on Troy's face. "Whooppeeee! Cookies!"

David snaked an arm around Troy's waist as he attempted to slip past him. "Whoa! First, bath time."

"Awww, Uncle David!"

"Grandma Louise's orders," David stated as he carried him away.

"Oh, okay then."

David laughed and wished every argument went so smoothly.

*   *   *

After bathing Riggs and herself, Sophie tried her dad's cell and her parents' house phone, but only got the answering machines. She left a message so they'd know she'd returned the call.

She plopped down on a bar stool to wait for David to bring Troy over. She had to admit that at first the idea had scared her. What did she know about kids? But then she'd looked into David's eyes and saw how much he needed a break, and all her reservations went out the proverbial window.

"It won't work, you know." Sophie rested her elbow on the counter, her chin in her palm, and watched Grandma wheeling herself around the kitchen. She was gathering baking supplies and piling them on the dining room table.

"What won't?"

"You trying to fix me up with David."

The affronted look on Grandma's face was almost believable. "Why ever would you think I was trying to do that?"

She snickered. "It's not like you're being very subtle."

"Bah." Grandma took a set of measuring spoons out of a drawer and set them on the counter. "What's wrong with hoping you'll find a nice young man and settle down?"

She arched an eyebrow. "I don't want to settle down."

"But you can't spend your whole life traveling the world. Alone." Grandma pushed the chair to the refrigerator. She pulled the door open slightly, but the chair prevented her from getting inside.

Sophie hopped off the stool and went to help her. "Why not?"

Grandma backed up the wheelchair. "Because one day you'll wake up old and lonely."

Heart aching, Sophie hugged her grandma. "Oh, Grams. I'm sorry."

She patted Grandma's back.

"I miss your grandfather so much, but I have never regretted the life we shared," Grandma said. "I just want you to have that. To know what it is to be loved by someone so completely."

Sophie felt a pang deep inside. She straightened. "I've tried. It didn't go so well."

"Those were boys. You need a man." Grandma wagged her eyebrows. "Don't you think David is handsome?"

Yes. But she wouldn't admit it out loud. "Grandma, you're impossible."

"Says you. I knew the minute I met David that you and he would be a good match."

Sophie groaned. "I knew it. You could've managed without me."

Grandma shook her head. "That's not totally true. I can't walk, after all. I'm stuck in this chair. How would I get ready for Christmas like this? I did want your help, and I like having you here. I couldn't travel to visit your parents this year. I didn't want to be alone, and I knew you might not go home for Christmas, so . . ."

Sophie hugged her grandma tight. "I love you."

"And I love you." Grandma spun and headed to the pantry. "I know I have a tub of cookie cutters in here."

"What did you need out of the fridge?" Sophie asked.

"Butter and eggs." She returned with a large, round plastic tub full of metal cookie cutters in various shapes.

"Will you teach me to make your persimmon cookies while I'm here?" One of her favorite treats from Christmases past was the persimmon cookies Grandma would send to California. Her brothers never cared for them, much to Sophie's delight. That meant she got to eat them all.

"I haven't made persimmon cookies in ages." Grandma's eyes crinkled at the corners. "They would make a lovely dessert for Friday night."

Sophie cocked her head. "Friday night?"

"Didn't I mention I've invited Simon to dinner?" Grandma smoothed a lock of silvery hair behind her ear. "He'd like to meet you."

Hmmm. Okay. "No, you didn't mention it, but that would be nice. What else should we serve?"

"Simon's not fussy when it comes to food," Grams assured her with a grin.

Sophie's eyebrows rose. "Really? So you and he have been see-ing each other for a while then?"

"What?" Grandma's eyes grew round. "Oh, no. We're not *seeing* each other. I couldn't . . . I mean, I'm not."

Nearly bursting with delight at the thought of her grandma no longer "waking up old and alone," as she put it, Sophie reached over to pat Grandma's hand and said, "Yes, you could, Grams."

Grandma's free hand went to her throat and her complexion paled. "It's not like that. We're only friends. We serve on the same committees at church and I only know his eating habits because we have a potluck every Sunday night. The man eats anything and everything. He says it's because he eats frozen dinners the rest of the week." Her face softened. "Poor man."

Sophie's mouth twitched with a smile. Grandma protested just a tad too enthusiastically. And that wasn't pity in her eyes. She cared for this man. "Does he have any family close by?"

"No. His only son's family lives in another state. We have that in common." Grandma averted her gaze, but not before Sophie saw the flash of pain in her eyes.

Sophie winced. Now that she was aware of Grandma's loneliness, Sophie was determined to make sure her parents and siblings knew as well. She made a mental note to call home tonight before she went to sleep. "I look forward to meeting Simon," she said. "We could make your sour cream enchiladas."

Her mouth watered even as she said the words. Though her mother had attempted on numerous occasions to replicate Grandma's recipe, they never tasted the same. After a while, her mother gave up cooking altogether and left meal preparation to Mrs. Lanohan, the housekeeper.

Sophie's stomach grumbled. It was past time for lunch. "After we make cookies I'll go to the grocery store. I could bring back a roasted chicken for dinner tonight."

She often grabbed food on the go when she was at her small studio apartment in Burbank, and roasted chicken was one of her favorites. Not that she'd been home for more than a day or two in the past few months. Her photography had finally gained some recognition, and clients had been coming out of the woodwork to hire her and her camera. Like this skiwear company. Every time she thought about it, she got excited.

"The groceries can wait until tomorrow," Grandma said. "Check the meat drawer. There's steak and chicken that need to be cooked, as well as some vegetables. And there's basmati rice in the cupboard. But first we need lunch. PB and J?"

"Yes. I haven't had a peanut butter and jelly sandwich since I was a kid." After rooting around in the pantry for a jar of peanut butter and raspberry jelly, she made them each a thick sandwich on whole wheat bread. The sweet and salty flavors made her long for those childhood summer days she'd spent with her grandparents. Lazy, carefree days. Grandpa would make fresh lemonade to go with their lunch and they'd go out into the backyard to enjoy the temperate sunshine.

Just as they were finishing up their lunch, a sharp rap at the door drew her attention. Riggs jumped up from his cushy bed beneath the front window and loped to the door.

"You answer the door while I clear the table," Grandma said, balancing their plates on her lap.

"I can get them, Grams," Sophie protested.

Grandma waved her away.

Riggs barked once and threw a glance over his shoulder at her. Really? The dog was impatient? "I'm coming."

Giving the pup a wry shake of her head, Sophie unlocked the bolt and opened the door to find a freshly washed Troy and David standing there.

"Hello," she said.

Riggs ran toward Troy, nearly knocking the child off his feet. Troy knelt down to hug the dog. Not a speck of mud remained in the layers of Troy's dark hair. His clothes were clean but baggy, as if the child had lost some weight.

Empathy squeezed her insides. The child's world had been turned inside out by his parents' tragic deaths. No doubt he was struggling to eat and sleep, and if his actions today were any indications, he was struggling to adjust to his new life with his uncle.

She was glad to see Troy taking comfort from Riggs. She wondered . . . when she left, maybe Troy would take Riggs?

Her gaze bounced to David. Her stomach muscles tightened at

the sight of his damp, slicked back hair, his strong jaw shadowed with just enough stubble to be fashionable but not scruffy. He was so handsome in his khakis, navy peacoat, and loafers. He just needed a red scarf wrapped around his neck and a jaunty driver hat on his head. She could see the image on the pages of a fashion catalog.

"Reporting for cookie making." His steel gray eyes roamed over her, from her loose hair to her sock-clad feet. The appreciation in his eyes left her feeling a bit tongue-tied.

"Wonderful." Self-consciously, she tugged at the hem of her lightweight wool shirt, making sure it hadn't ridden up over the top of her jeans. Where were her manners? She stepped back. "Please come in."

David ushered Troy inside so Sophie could shut the door. Riggs moved into the living room and Troy followed.

"Troy, so good to see you." Grandma opened her arms for a quick hug. Troy went easily into her arms. "Look how handsome you are all spiffed up."

"How is he?" Sophie asked David in a hushed voice.

"Calmer," David admitted as he tracked Troy with his gaze. "It's been a rough six months."

"I can only imagine," she whispered. "Both of your lives have been derailed."

He ran a hand over his jaw. "We've definitely been set on a different path."

She liked his optimistic outlook. "It can't be easy becoming a parent in the blink of an eye."

"It hasn't been," he admitted. "Thankfully, your grandmother has been here to offer advice and support."

"That is a blessing," she said. "Learning to parent on the fly has to be difficult. Most people have months to plan and prepare.

I admire you for taking Troy into your home." She ached with sympathy for all they'd endured.

"Thank you." He met her eyes, his gaze boring into her as if he could see all the way to the secret places she kept hidden from the world. It was a dizzying sensation.

"I appreciated the help this morning," he said in a quiet tone. His words rippled over her like warm honey.

"What are neighbors for?" she quipped, hoping to lighten the tension that had suddenly sprung up between them.

"Right." Something in his tone made her think he was ill at ease.

She studied him closely. "Having second thoughts about leaving him with us?"

He cringed. "It's just that he can be a handful."

She followed his gaze to where Grandma was showing Troy the baking supplies. "You don't have to worry. Between the two of us we can handle him for a few hours." She hoped.

He took her hand. Warmth raced up her arm. "I do appreciate this. I'll pay you back."

She squeezed his hand and tugged him to the front door. "You don't owe us a thing. This will be fun for Grams." She opened the door. "Now, go get some work done."

* * *

"Are they finished yet?" Troy hunched in front of the oven to watch the last batch of cookies turn golden on the cookie sheet.

Sophie glanced at the timer. "Two more minutes." She brushed her fingers through his hair, dislodging a few stray, colorful sprinkles. "We may not get to decorate these. Your uncle should be here any second."

She'd been saying that for the past thirty minutes. In the past two hours, they'd made four batches of sugar cookies, using every single cookie cutter in Grandma's tub. There was frosting on the walls. A light dusting of flour coated the kitchen's hardwood floor. But Grandma was having a blast. And so was she.

Troy was a delight. He made the time fly by with his chatter and laughter. He had so many questions. And he was smart and imaginative, too. Not once had he thrown any sort of tantrum or quibbled when Grandma or Sophie had corrected him—not even when they'd told him not to put frosting on Riggs's food.

Except it was past the time for David to return. Sophie hoped nothing had happened to him. She'd found the number he left and called his cell. After three rings it went to voice mail. Hmmm. Had he fallen asleep? She'd give him another half hour, then she'd go over there.

The timer dinged.

"Done!" Troy hollered and danced around the kitchen, slipping slightly in the flour.

"Careful," Grandma warned from the dining room table. She had a dollop of frosting on her cheek and her eyes sparkled.

"Okay, little man, stand back." Sophie slipped on an oven mitt and opened the oven door. A wall of heat hit her in the face, making her hair curl. She blew a loose strand out of her eyes as she removed the cookie tray and set it on the stove, and then quickly used a spatula to transfer the cookies to the wire rack. "Now we have to wait for a few minutes for them to cool."

"I don't like waiting," Troy huffed. "Everything is always about waiting. Wait for school to start. Wait for Uncle David to pick me up. Wait for my favorite show. Wait for the cookies. Wait. Wait. Wait."

Sophie suppressed a smile and knelt down to look Troy in the eye. How could she explain the concept of patience to a child? "I know waiting can be hard sometimes. And you feel frustrated by having to wait. Is that what happened when you ran away to the park?"

His chin dropped and he made circles in the flour with his toe. "Uncle David said we'd go to the park. He wanted to wait until after lunch. But I was tired of waiting."

"Maybe next time you have to wait and if you feel yourself becoming frustrated you could sing a song." Sophie wasn't sure where that idea came from but she went with it. "Do you have a favorite song?"

Troy nodded. "'Baby Beluga.'"

"I don't know that one. Can you sing it for me?"

Quietly, he started to sing the song about a baby whale in the deep blue sea. At first she had to strain to hear him, but his voice got louder as he went along. Partway through, his voice faltered as he reached a verse that talked about the whale's mommy. Tears welled in Troy's eyes and rolled down his cheeks.

Sophie's heart sputtered as she pulled the child into her arms. "Oh, baby, I'm sorry. I didn't mean to make you sad."

"I miss my mommy."

"I know you do, honey." She rubbed his back and felt tears prick her eyes.

"I want Uncle David." He tightened his hold on her. "You don't think anything bad has happened to him, too, do you?"

His words pierced her. "Oh, no. I'm sure he's fine." She glanced at the clock again, and sent up a silent prayer that what she said was true, even as a slow, burning anger simmered low in her gut. Poor Troy was terrified that something bad had happened to his uncle. David had to realize he couldn't be so insensitive to his nephew's fragile state of mind.

She leaned back to look into Troy's face. Using her thumbs, she wiped away his tears. "Why don't you help Grandma put all the cookie cutters back in the tub while I run next door to see what's keeping your uncle."

Troy sniffled and nodded. "Okay."

Sharing a concerned glance with Grams, Sophie lifted Troy onto the chair next to Grandma. "I'll be right back."

She grabbed her coat and traded her slippers for Grandma's tall rain boots and marched outside, ready to give David Murphy a piece of her mind.

CHAPTER 4

Insistent tapping forced David to lift his hands from the keyboard and jerk his gaze away from the computer screen. He blinked as his eyes adjusted to the darkened house. He'd been so deeply lost in his work he hadn't noticed that night had fallen.

Disoriented, David struggled to make sense of what was happening. He'd heard a noise. But now the house was eerily quiet.

His hands ached, his shoulder muscles throbbed.

What time was it?

He hit the button on his phone to check the time. His stomach dropped. Oh, man. He was more than an hour late picking up his nephew.

And Sophie had called. Twice.

He'd put his phone on *do not disturb* after having talked to everyone at work, putting out fires that needed his attention. He should have set an alarm. He knew that. But he'd been so focused on pushing through, trying to get this app done, that he'd forgotten. And Troy had paid the price.

The sharp rap against the glass windowpane behind him drew him from his chair. He pushed aside the curtain and came face-to-face with a shadowy figure. Startled, he stumbled back, tripping over the chair and landing on the floor on all fours. Would a burglar knock?

"David!"

Sophie.

Heart thumping, he jumped up and pushed the curtain aside again, but she was gone. He had to get to Louise's. What if something had happened to Troy? He didn't think he could handle any more tragedies. He'd had his fill, thank you very much.

A few seconds later, knocking at the front door had him picking his way through the land mines of toys. He flipped on the porch light and opened the door. Sophie stood on the other side with her hands on her hips and her mouth pressed into a grim line.

His heart squeezed tight and alarm sped through his veins. "Is Troy okay?"

"Yes. He's okay now. But he's worried about his uncle."

Shadows played across the planes of her face, hiding her eyes, but there was no mistaking the sharp-edged tone of her voice. Uh-oh. He was in deep trouble with the lovely lady. As he should be. He'd let her down. He hated that feeling. He owed her so much and could never thank her and Louise enough for inviting Troy over to bake Christmas cookies.

Even though he knew Sophie had agreed to allow Troy to impose for Louise's sake, it was really nice of her to be so accommodating. She'd come to Bellevue to be with her grandmother, not to entertain a five-year-old. "I'm so sorry. I totally lost track of time. I'll come over right now and get him."

"You turned your phone off." The accusation hung in the air like wisps of smoke.

He blew out a breath that turned white in the cold air. "I made the mistake of checking in at the office," he said. "Then my employees kept calling me back, so I put it on *do not disturb*. I wasn't thinking. Here, let me grab my jacket and we can go to your grandma's."

Instead of answering, she glided past him to enter the dark house.

"Wait!" he warned as he reached for the light switch.

When the light came on, she stood frozen in the middle of the Thomas the Train track with her foot stuck inside the Knapford Station. Her arms were out to her sides, like she was about to take flight. The ponytail sticking out the back of her hat swished as she whipped her gaze to him. She was so cute.

"Do you mind?" she prompted.

Suppressing a grin, he rushed to release her foot before she crushed the plastic and wooden piece. He reattached the station to the track. "Sorry."

With one hand, David grabbed a robotic dinosaur with a stuffed dog in its mouth, and with his other hand he cleared a path through the pile of Lego pieces. She navigated her way through the rest of the land mines and stopped by the dining room table. She surveyed his home with just the barest hint of a raised eyebrow.

He glanced around, seeing the place from her point of view. It was a complete mess. It looked like the toy box had barfed all over the house. Only they didn't have a toy box. Note to self: buy a toy box.

The train track took up the entryway and crept into the space that divided the dining and living rooms. Train pieces littered the rug. A dump truck carrying building blocks sat on the back of the couch, where Troy had been playing last night before bed. A haphazard stack of books looked like it was about to topple off the coffee table. "We're not too tidy around here."

She considered him for a moment. "No, you're not. Why is that?"

He opened his mouth to answer but realized he only had excuses. He was too tired at the end of the day to pick up. It was easier to leave everything where it was, since Troy would only drag it all out again anyway. He settled for a shrug.

"Look," she said in a modulated tone, "you've got to prioritize your life differently. Troy has to come first. If you can't hire a nanny, then you need to work when he sleeps."

David ran a hand through his hair. He was exhausted. And he didn't need a lecture. "Yeah. You're right. I can do a lot when he's in bed. It's just—"

"Just what?"

He cringed at the sharp edge to her tone. "He has nightmares."

Her expression softened. "That's rough."

He'd survived on little sleep in college; he could do so for two weeks. "And there are some things I can only accomplish during normal business hours. I have a company to run."

Her eyes widened. "You own your company. Okay. I get it." A dose of derision filled her lovely face. "I do. My parents were like that. Workaholics. It left my brothers and me feeling very disconnected and unimportant."

He ached for the hurt he heard in her voice. He didn't want Troy to feel that way, but what was he to do? He didn't have a partner to share the load of parenting with. Though from the sound of it, both of Sophie's parents put work ahead of their children. "By summer I can hire a nanny. But that doesn't solve the immediate problem."

"Don't you have employees who can take care of business for a while? What do you do when you go on vacation?"

"I've never gone on vacation."

Her brows hitched to her hairline. "Ever?"

Uncomfortable under her incredulous stare, he moved to his desk to save his work. "Not in the five years since I started my company. Not counting the time after Daniel and Beth's accident. Troy and I were both a mess then."

And he hadn't taken a vacation before that either, but he wasn't about to share that tidbit. Growing up, money had been beyond tight. Day trips to the beach or hiking had been the extent of their family vacations. Then came college, and he'd worked as well as studied.

"Maybe you should consider taking a vacation for the next two weeks while Troy is out of school," she suggested.

He considered her words. What would a vacation look like? It wouldn't be a real vacation, since he wouldn't be leaving town. Didn't they call that a staycation? "I don't know if I can do that."

She stepped closer. Her expression puzzled. "You don't trust your employees?"

"I do," he was quick to assure her. "It's not that. I don't know if I"—he thumped his chest—"could take time away from work." He glanced at his computer. All that still needed to be done on his project raced through his mind. "If I tell you what I'm working on, will you promise not to tell anyone?"

She widened her eyes and canted her head. "Of course. Who would I tell?"

"There are people out there who would love to get their hands on my computations."

"And you think I'm one of them?" She laughed.

Excited to share his vision with her, he explained his idea for a finger sensor on electronic device platforms to monitor hydration levels. "Do you see how this might be a useful app?"

Enthusiasm brightened her face as she looked at his design. "Yeah. I'm so impressed. If you can pull this off, your app could help the elderly, athletes . . . everyone. Water is such an important part of our lives."

He couldn't stop the way his chest expanded with her praise. "I wish I could say I was the one to first think up the idea. But I might be the first to actually make it happen."

"So that's what you're working on here." She pointed to the desk.

"Yes."

"Then you don't need to go into the office?"

"I haven't the past two days, but I've got meetings scheduled for Wednesday, Thursday, and Friday."

"What are you planning to do with Troy?"

Acid churned in his stomach. That was a quandary he'd been wrestling with for the past week. "I'll have to take him with me."

"Can you reschedule the appointments until after the holidays?"

He shook his head. "No. Each meeting is with a big client. I can't afford to put them off. I need to secure the business before the end of the year."

She tugged on her bottom lip with her teeth. She seemed to be struggling with something. Her gaze moved to the table. She let out a small gasp and picked up his sketchbook.

He sucked in a sharp breath. The etching he'd drawn of her stared back at her from the pages of the sketchbook.

"You did this?" She lifted her luminous eyes to stare at him.

He straightened. Oh, no. He hoped she didn't think that was strange. "I'm sorry, I hope you don't mind—"

"It's beautiful," she said.

She was beautiful, he thought. But what he said was, "I studied art as well as computer science in college."

"Where did you go?"

"DigiPen in Redmond, Washington." The technology school was world renowned in the gaming and software world.

"You're good." She continued to stare at her image. "I could watch Troy for you while you take your meetings."

Wait. Did she just say what he thought she said? "You'd do that?"

Setting the sketchbook back on the table, she lifted her chin. "Yes, if you promise to take the rest of the two weeks off."

"Wow. I don't know what to say."

"Say yes. Troy needs you right now. This will be the first Christmas without his parents."

The reminder punched him in the gut. The burn of grief stung his eyes. He blinked rapidly to banish the tears. "Yes. Christmas will be hard. For both of us."

She touched his arm. "I'm sorry. Of course you're grieving, too. Maybe you need the time off for yourself as well."

Touched by her concern, he put his hand over hers. "I'll take that into consideration."

She slipped her hand from beneath his. "Okay, now that that is settled, we should head to Grandma's."

As she stepped past him, he snagged her hand and drew her closer. The glow from the dining room ceiling lamp sparked in her eyes, highlighting the crystal blue irises rimmed in a darker hue of blue. A man could lose himself in those serene pools of color and light. "Thank you. I can't tell you how blessed Troy and I are to have you and Louise in our lives."

Her breath hitched slightly. She licked her lips. He tracked the movement, and his gut clenched. "We're happy to help you out."

He wanted to kiss her. The thought tore through him like a flash of lightning. Yearning built in his chest. He felt a magnetic pull toward her.

He knew he should resist. Knew it wouldn't be smart or gentlemanly to give in to the desire to kiss her. He leaned toward her and managed by sheer will to stop halfway, allowing her the choice to close the distance between them or to turn away. He hoped she would close the distance.

She ducked her head and tugged her hand free, then stepped around him. "Uh, Troy's waiting."

He straightened but couldn't speak. His tongue was glued to the roof of his mouth as humiliation flooded his system.

What had he been thinking?

She was way out of his league. A world traveler, a sophisticated photographer who probably had rich, good-looking men falling over themselves trying to gain her attention.

He gave a mental snort. That's the thing. He hadn't been thinking. Apparently that was today's theme. Wow! For a smart man, he was acting like an idiot.

❄   ❄   ❄

Sophie's pulse pounded in her ears as she hurried across the driveway toward Grandma's house. David was right behind her. She could feel his presence in the prickling of her skin and her heightened senses. His musky scent wrapped around her, chasing away the chill of the December evening.

She tried not to think about what had just happened, but the memory wouldn't leave her mind. First she'd found the charcoal drawing. Was that really how he saw her? She'd been flattered and flabbergasted.

Then to realize David wanted to kiss her . . .

And had nearly done so, but then he hadn't. He'd hovered just out of reach, like forbidden fruit.

At first she'd been confused and hurt, thinking he'd suddenly realized what he was about to do and had changed his mind. But then she'd realized he was letting her make the choice whether to kiss him.

Why, oh why, hadn't she kissed him?

She wanted to. Ached with the desire to press her lips to his. To feel his arms around her and to snuggle close to him. But it wouldn't be wise. Right now, she and David were both in strange places in their lives. She was on the cusp of realizing a dream and he was struggling to figure out how to parent his nephew while running his company. It would be far too easy to get caught up in the feelings bouncing around her heart and head. Too easy to think that this handsome man could be the "one," as Grandma hoped.

Sophie wasn't sure there was a "one" out there for her. Someone who would accept her, flaws and all. She wasn't even sure she wanted to find the one—not if it meant giving up her dream job or her career.

No, she needed to keep things between her and David on a neighborly basis. Friends. Especially since she would be caring for Troy. The last thing Troy needed was to get his hopes up that she and David would ever be together. She was leaving after New Year's for the job she'd been working toward her whole life, and nothing short of a natural disaster could keep her away from that.

With that thought, she opened Grandma's front door and ush-ered David inside. Troy scrambled down from the dining room table and raced across the living room to launch himself into David's arms.

David held his nephew against his chest. "I'm sorry I'm late, buddy."

"I thought—" Troy buried his face in David's neck.

"I'm right here," David cooed. "And you were safe with Louise and Sophie."

Troy nodded and leaned back. His eyes shone with tears and his lip quivered. "We made Christmas cookies. Though some of the shapes aren't Christmasy but I put red and green frosting on them. Now they look like Christmas. I made a tiger and a bear and the waffle tower."

Sophie chuckled. "*Eiffel* Tower."

"That's so exciting." David set Troy on his feet and gave Sophie a tight smile. "We'll get out of your hair now."

Grandma rolled up, nudging Sophie aside without so much as a how do you do. Sophie eyed Grandma with suspicion.

"David, we'd love for you and Troy to stay for dinner," Grams stated firmly. "Troy and I were just about to watch a Christmas movie."

Sophie should have seen that coming.

"Yes! Please, Uncle David!" Troy hopped up and down like his feet were spring-loaded.

Riggs barked and danced around Troy, excited by the child's excitement.

Grandma beamed, and Sophie's heart clenched. The com-pany was good for Grandma. And if Sophie hoped to convince David that he and Troy should give Riggs a home, she needed

him to be around the dog more and to see how good Riggs was
for Troy.

She'd just have to put her own confused and scattered feelings aside.

David met Sophie's gaze. She could see hesitation in his eyes.
After rebuffing his kiss, he no doubt thought she didn't want him
around. "We'd love to have you stay."

She meant it. David intrigued her. And if they were to become
friends, she wanted to know more about him. His selflessness
in taking in his nephew said a lot about his character. Not many
single guys she knew would have made the sacrifice.

One corner of David's mouth curved. "Four to one. I guess the
answer is yes."

"Four?" Sophie cantered her head in confusion.

David's gaze dropped to the dog, who now lay on the floor at
Troy's feet, his big head resting on his paws and his dark eyes
twinkling. David chuckled. "How could anyone resist him?"

Sophie grinned. "How indeed." She moved to step over Riggs
just as the dog lifted to his feet, setting Sophie off balance. Her
arms windmilled as she toppled toward the floor. Years of gymnas-
tics as a kid kicked into gear and she tucked and rolled, landing
on her feet in a squat.

She jumped up and turned to stare at Grandma. "That's how
you hurt your foot, isn't it?"

Grandma's eyes were huge and her mouth open with astonishment before she clamped her lips together and smiled sheepishly.
"Maybe."

"Note to self," Sophie said. "Don't try to walk over Riggs or
you'll end up on the floor."

Riggs let out a bark and then licked her hand.

"Wow, that was impressive," David said, amusement lacing his words. "What do you call that move?"

"A somersault."

"Show me how to do that!" Troy attempted to roll on the floor but rolled off his shoulder and landed with a thud on his backside. Sophie ignored David's interested stare and proceeded to teach Troy how to do a proper somersault.

CHAPTER 5

With Louise and Troy in the living room watching a Christmas movie, David leaned against the kitchen counter. He watched Sophie pulling food from the refrigerator. She'd tied a green-and-red-striped apron around her waist. Trading the rain boots for fuzzy slippers, she'd retied her pretty hair up with a bright yellow hair band, revealing the long, slender column of her neck.

He could see the pulse point just above the collar of her shirt and couldn't help wondering if he would feel her pulse jump if he placed a kiss there.

Considering her reaction the last time he'd attempted to kiss her, he stayed where he was. Still, it didn't hurt to wonder, did it? He could feel his ears turning red. Hopefully, she'd think it was the warmth of the house. If she even noticed. She'd hardly looked at him since he'd agreed to stay for dinner. Not that he blamed her. He'd acted impulsively. There was a reason he didn't usually do that.

He noted she wore no jewelry. She didn't need any. She was pretty without any decorations. It had been a long time since he'd been this attracted to a woman. Not since Sybil. His college girlfriend.

They'd met his first year. She'd worked in the coffee shop near the campus and had an exotic beauty, with dark, short, spiky hair and coffee-colored, almond-shaped eyes. They'd dated for a year before she'd moved on to follow her dream of being a flight attendant. He'd never heard from her again.

Her rejection had fueled his frantically paced schedule the next few years. He hadn't wanted to admit he'd thought she hadn't believed in him and his dream of opening his own software company. But in the end, she'd left him, just like everyone else. He'd wanted to prove to her, to his parents, to everyone, that he would succeed without anyone else's help.

Strange, he hadn't thought about Sybil in years. With time and perspective, he realized he hadn't been heartbroken, just indignant, when she'd left. But that hurt was long gone, as were his feelings for her.

Forcing his thoughts away from the past, he focused on the lovely woman in front of him. "What can I do to help?"

"Not sure yet." Sophie laid everything on the counter and surveyed her bounty of broccoli, carrots, and a package of uncooked chicken. "Will Troy eat broccoli?"

"I don't know." Guilt squeezed him. Shouldn't he know something like that about the boy? Anxiety ate at him. "We've been surviving on prepackaged foods with some fruit thrown in for nutrition. I guess I should make more of an effort to cook real food."

Sophie laughed. "You'll figure it out. Give yourself time. Now that you're taking some time off, you could buy a cookbook and experiment."

He laughed. "Only if you promise to eat what I make."

She slanted him a startled glance. "Uh, well, uh, okay. I'm sure Grandma and I would be happy to taste test your creations."

He'd flustered her again. It was easy to do. And he had to admit he liked the way her nose crinkled up in confusion and her eyes grew wide. He liked her.

There. He'd admitted it to himself. No harm in that. They needed to be friends. She was going to be a part of his and Troy's lives for the next few days at least, and he'd better like and trust her if he were going to leave Troy with her.

He'd just have to be careful not to let himself or Troy become too attached to the pretty photographer.

She pushed up the sleeves of her off-white shirt. "Would you mind firing up the oven to four twenty-five? I'll roast the chicken with some diced potatoes and carrots and steam the broccoli."

"Sounds good." He did as he was asked. "I can cut up the potatoes."

She handed him a cutting board. "Knives are in the center drawer."

Glad to have something to do, he set out to chop the potatoes into cubes. "Louise said you grew up in Hollywood."

"Actually, my parents' home is in West Hollywood." She washed the chicken and patted it dry with a paper towel. "Though they work in Hollywood."

"Doing what?"

"A little of everything behind the camera. Scriptwriting, producing, directing." She turned her interested gaze on him. "Where did you grow up?"

His stomach clenched. He should have expected the question. He didn't like talking about his childhood. "Eastern Washington. Will you be heading south for Christmas Day?"

If she noticed how quickly he changed the subject she didn't let on. "Nope, I'm planning on staying here with Grandma until after New Year's. I never know from year to year if I'll make it home for the holidays. My parents have so much going on at this time of year, they hardly notice my absence, and my brothers all have their own families now." She placed the chicken in a glass pan. "Hopefully, Grandma will be walking by then."

"No doubt Louise will love having you stay," he said. He'd assumed she'd go home for Christmas, then fly off to the job she had waiting for her. He couldn't deny he was glad to hear Sophie would be around for a little while longer than he'd thought. Not that he planned on spending any more time with her than necessary. "It's nice that you have a flexible job."

"It's not great on my pocketbook, but Grandma needs me, and I'm happy to be here with her while I have the time."

"Did you have to give up a photography job to be here?"

"No. Thankfully, I was just wrapping up one in Gran Canaria, so the timing couldn't have been better."

"Ah, that explains the tan."

She flashed him a grin. It was like the sun coming out on a spring day. "Yes. It was a bit of a shock to come from the balmy Canary Islands to here." She added diced carrots to the chicken. "I'm sure my agent would have found me a Christmas shoot with a magazine or something. She's the best in the business."

"Only the best for the best." He slid the cubed potato pieces into the pan and watched as she poured olive oil and seasonings over the food.

She let out a wry laugh. "Right." She moved past him to grab a stack of plates from a cupboard. "What about your family? Are your parents still in eastern Washington?"

"No." He took the plates from her and set them on the

counter. "You must be thrilled at the prospect of going abroad again."

"I am. This job will add more prestige as well as photos to my portfolio, and if they like my work they'll probably hire me for more."

"Which reminds me, I'd still love to see your portfolio. Did you bring it with you?"

Her cheeks flushed. From the oven's heat or a blush? "You can see it online. I have the hard copy of my portfolio in my studio in Burbank."

"Oh, you have a studio? For portraits?" He hadn't thought she did studio sittings.

"No." She crinkled up her nose. "I mean, I do portraits, but not in a studio. I meant my studio apartment. I use it mostly for storage and as a staging area."

"I see. I lived in a studio in downtown Bellevue for years. In a high-rise. It was, well, very different from the suburbs."

She opened a drawer and pulled out silverware.

"You miss your life before Troy?"

He frowned, darting a quick glance toward the living room. Just in case Troy could hear, he dropped his voice. "Life has certainly changed." He shrugged. "It is what it is. Before I was alone, and now I have Troy." And thanks to this amazing and beautiful woman, Troy was safe and would be cared for when David was at work this week.

He needed to change the subject before he said something like that out loud. "Hey, so Troy and I are going to buy a Christmas tree tonight." He'd been trying to think of a way to make it up to her, and this seemed like it might work. "I noticed that Louise doesn't have one. I'd like to repay you for everything you've done. Can I pick up one for you guys while we're there?"

Sophie tucked in her chin. "You don't have to repay me."

He held her gaze with determination. "I always repay my debts."

"I appreciate the offer, but I can take care of it."

She sounded insulted. Not at all what he'd meant to accomplish. But he couldn't accept her charity. Even well-intentioned charity. "I know you're capable of doing it, but I'd like to."

A frown marred her forehead. "My help doesn't come with a price tag."

Definitely offended. "I know it doesn't. I didn't mean to imply it did. But I have a truck. I'll be bringing a tree home for my house, and just thought I could bring you a Christmas tree, too."

Grandma called from the living room. "We're going Christmas tree shopping? How fun!"

He shared an *uh-oh* look with Sophie. Apparently Louise had been listening to their conversation. Hopefully, Troy wasn't as adept at eavesdropping.

"I'm planning on picking up a couple of fir trees from the lot at the grocers," he said as he stepped into the living room. If Sophie wouldn't accept his offer, then he'd go through Louise to get his way. "I owe Sophie big time for all her help."

❄   ❄   ❄

Sophie arched an eyebrow at his retreating back. He was serious about making restitution. That didn't sit well with her. But it also made her curious why he'd feel the need. Why couldn't he accept help without feeling an obligation to reciprocate?

"Uncle David!" Troy protested. "My mom said the good trees come from farms."

Hearing Troy talk of his mother compelled Sophie to hurry

forward. If the child cried again, she wanted to be there for him. But even as that thought formed, she reminded herself it wasn't her place to comfort Troy.

"All Christmas trees come from tree farms, Troy," Sophie said, joining them. She eyed Troy carefully. He didn't appear to be on the verge of tears. "The ones at lots are usually sold as fund-raisers for various clubs or charities. So it's not a bad thing to buy from the grocery store."

"But it's much more enjoyable to go to a tree farm and cut down your own tree," Grandma interjected. "Your grandfather and I went to school with the family who owns and operates Sleigh Bells tree farm. They have plenty of attractions that make the experience fun. They've got a petting zoo, a Santa House, and sleigh rides."

"And cinnamon-covered donuts!" Troy let out a whoop. "Last year we watched them make the donuts and then got to eat them while they were hot. Yummm."

Sophie's heart was warmed to see that Troy had such a fond memory to hold on to.

"Let's do it!" Grandma clapped her hands in joy.

"Grams, it's raining," Sophie protested. Someone had to be the practical one. "Not to mention cold."

"You do remember you're in the Pacific Northwest, right?" David asked. An amused smile tugged at the corners of his mouth. "Rainy and cold is what winter is about here."

She couldn't argue that point. "But the tree will be too wet to put up." Sophie imagined the mess that would be. Water droplets all over the place.

"That will be true wherever the Christmas tree comes from," David countered. "It will have to dry in the garage until you're ready to decorate, either way."

"That makes too much sense," Sophie replied with a wry laugh. "But Grandma shouldn't be out and about in the dark, rainy night."

"Hey, I'm not an invalid," Grandma said. "I can wheel myself through trees. And it doesn't require standing to munch on warm donuts."

"We haven't even had dinner yet," Sophie said with a pointed look at her grandmother.

Grandma waved a hand. "After dinner, silly."

"Can Riggs come, too?" Troy asked as he plopped down next to the puppy for some love.

"Does the Christmas tree farm allow pets?" Sophie asked Grams.

"I believe so."

Sophie glanced at the clock. "How late is the farm open?"

"Good question," David said and pulled his cell phone from his pocket. "I'll find out. Hopefully they have their hours posted on their website. What was the name of the place?"

"Sleigh Bells."

He grimaced as he looked at the screen. "They're only open until eight. By the time we eat and drive there, we wouldn't have much time to look for a tree."

Seeing the disappointment on Troy's face and in Grandma's eyes, Sophie gave in. "Let's make a day of it on Saturday, then. We could ride the sleigh, eat donuts, and pick a tree."

"And pet the animals!" Troy cheered. "What about Riggs?"

"Let's see." David scrolled through the screen on the phone. "Yes. They allow dogs on leash."

"Yay!" Troy hugged Riggs. "Hear that, boy? You get to come with us."

Riggs barked and gave Troy a slobbery kiss.

Sophie laughed and her heart swelled. She liked this. Liked being here with David and Troy and Grandma. She turned away and reminded herself not to get used to it. She was leaving after New Year's. But the normal excitement she felt when she thought about traveling, of seeing a new place and photographing new wonders, didn't make her pulse pound.

Instead, she felt a confusing pang of loss.

*   *   *

"Thank you, ladies, for a wonderful home-cooked meal," David said as he rubbed his full stomach. He'd eaten more than his fair share. Having existed on ready-made dishes for so long, this was a special treat. Almost as special as being here with Sophie and Louise.

"You helped, so you deserve some of the credit," Sophie said with a smile. She sat across from him in her grandmother's dining room. The light from the craftsman-style chandelier bounced off her shiny blond hair. He liked her delicately carved bone structure, the straight line of her nose, the curve of her cheek. Her face captured his interest, but there was more to her beauty. An inner vibrancy and vitality that made him itch to have a set of colored pencils and a sketch pad at his disposal.

He realized he was staring. He rose and gathered their plates. "Let Troy and me clear the table and do the dishes."

"I'm not done eating," Troy said around a mouthful of chicken. It seemed he, too, enjoyed the meal. Even the broccoli. David would have to remember to make the vegetable for dinner in the future.

"Leave the dishes for later," Louise said. "Troy and I have to finish our movie." Her blue eyes twinkled. "Riggs needs to be walked. Why don't you two take him out?"

"Grandma." Sophie arched an eyebrow at her grandmother. There was a note of warning in her tone. What was that about?

"Yes, dear?" Louise cocked her head at her granddaughter.

David wasn't sure what was going on between the two women and certainly didn't want to get in the middle of it.

"I don't mind taking Riggs out."

Sophie turned her gaze to him. There was speculation in her eyes. "Really? Okay. The dishes can wait, then."

"As soon as you're finished eating, Troy, we'll watch the rest of *It's a Wonderful Life*," Louise said.

Troy gobbled up the last of his potatoes and broccoli. "Done!"

Louise backed her wheelchair away from the dining room table. "Do you think Clarence will get his wings?"

Troy scrambled from the table. "I hope so."

Sophie whistled and Riggs jumped up from his bed. "Want to go for a walk, boy?"

The dog barked and trotted to the front door.

David laughed. "I take that as a yes."

"Seems so."

He and Sophie shared a smile. Warmth spread through him. Then she turned away and headed for the coat rack. David followed, disconcerted by his reaction to Sophie, and retrieved his jacket. Once they were bundled up and the leash attached to Riggs's collar, they headed outside. The cool air was a welcome relief from his inner turmoil.

As soon as they hit the sidewalk, Sophie handed him the leash. He expected Riggs to balk or pull at the lead but he walked happily by David's side.

The night was chilly and the air was moist, but thankfully the mist wasn't enough to deter them. They walked silently through the neighborhood. David wondered if Sophie felt as awkward as he did. Maybe small talk would ease the tension. "Seen any good movies lately?"

She glanced at him. With the moonlight hitting her face, he could see amusement in her eyes. "Yes, actually. On the plane."

She went on to tell him the plot of a sci-fi film with some big-name stars. He liked the melodic quality of her voice. It was soothing.

"Have you met any of those actors?" he asked. In her line of work she was bound to have rubbed elbows with celebrities.

"I have," she said, though there was a note of wariness in her tone.

"You must get that question a lot."

She sighed. "Yes, I do."

Since he wasn't that interested in famous people, he decided to switch topics. "I'm not much of a movie watcher. I prefer books."

"Who's your favorite author?"

He ran down the list of his top five writers and was pleased to discover she'd also read books by a couple of them, though she preferred lighter reading. They had a lively debate on the plot twists in a recent offering by one of their shared favorite authors.

When they reached the gate to the off-leash area of the nearby park, Riggs sat and stared expectantly at them.

"I didn't bring the tennis ball," Sophie said and stroked the dog's head. "Sorry, boy."

As if understanding, he rose and sniffed a trail to the play structure. Sophie sat on a swing.

David leaned against the slide and kept a grip on Riggs's leash. The dog was content to sniff the ground at the end of the lead. "I need to apologize for earlier," he said. "I'm sorry. I don't normally try to kiss pretty women I've only just met."

She sent the swing moving with the toe of her shoe. "I'm not sure how to respond to that. Thank you?"

"My only excuse is the stress I'm under," he continued, feeling the need to explain so she wouldn't think he was a total loser. "Between caring for Troy and work and my special project, I'm spread so thin. I lost my head there for a moment."

Her blue eyes glittered in the moonlight. "It's kind of gratifying to think I could make you lose your head."

He heard the laughter in her voice. "You're making fun of me."

"Maybe. I accept your apology and you don't need to feel bad about it. You have a lot on your plate."

He stared out at the trees. "Yes. Daniel would have handled it all with ease. He never let life rattle him."

"Grandma said they died in a car accident." Sophie's voice was soft and gentle.

Searing pain went through him, but he forged ahead with the story. "They were heading home from Seattle," he told her. "They'd taken Troy to the Space Needle and to the aquarium on the waterfront."

Sophie let out a small gasp. "Troy was with them?"

"Yes. He'd fallen asleep, and thankfully was strapped securely in his car seat when a drunk driver hit them head-on. They were headed home on the SR520 Bridge."

"The floating bridge? I thought there was a divider."

"Yeah, well, this clown got on the bridge going in the wrong direction. He smashed into Daniel's sedan."

"That's horrible."

"Daniel and Beth died within minutes of impact. At least that's what the police told me."

She rose and came to him. "And the driver of the other car?"

"He died as well." There was no solace in the man's death. It was so needless.

"No wonder Troy has nightmares." She touched a hand to his sleeve—lightly, but there was still a connection. "I can't imagine the sorrow you feel. Or the rage at the senselessness of the accident."

He straightened. She was so close, the scent of vanilla and sugar clinging to her hair wrapped around him, cocooning him in warmth. "No, I don't suppose many people could." He stared up at the moon. Raindrops hit his face. He didn't mind. He hoped the rain hid the tears that leaked from his eyes. "Daniel had asked me to go with them. He was always doing that, trying to include me. I'd declined because I was working on my project. I was always working, too busy for family."

"If you'd gone, you might have died, too."

Her words scored him clean through.

"What would have happened to Troy?" he said.

"Grandma says you and Troy attend her church occasionally," she said softly.

He sucked in a breath. He went for Troy's sake. "Yes. When we can get ourselves up and out the door in time."

She slid her hand down his arm until she captured his hand. "I hope you'll seek God's peace and comfort. He has a plan for you. And for Troy."

He threaded his fingers through hers and started walking back toward Louise's house, Riggs out in front of them, as a way to stall responding. Sophie had such a sweet nature. She was as optimistic as Daniel had been.

"I appreciate your words," he finally said. "But Daniel was the one who prayed and went to church. I go because I know that is what Daniel would want for Troy."

"It's noble of you to honor your brother in that way." She squeezed his hand. "Wouldn't Daniel want that for you, too?"

His heart twisted in his chest as her words dug in deep. "Yes, he would."

But just because he was going to church didn't mean he and God were on speaking terms. Not by a long shot.

❄   ❄   ❄

Late that night, Sophie called her parents again. Dad answered and immediately put her on speaker. "I'm here with your mother," Dad's voice filled Sophie's ear. "Where are you?"

"In Washington." She sat on the bed in the guest room and plucked at the thread nubbins on the comforter. "Did you know Grandma was injured?"

"What?" her mother cried. "How did that happen?"

Sophie hesitated before revealing the circumstances of her grandmother's injury. "Well, she tripped over her puppy."

"Why on earth would she get a dog?" Dad asked.

"She's lonely," Sophie replied, trying to keep censure from her tone.

"Why did she call you?" Mom asked. "Why are you there? I thought you were on some island paradise for a location shoot."

"I was. She called to see if I would come help her."

Her mother let out a huff. "If she needed help she should have called us."

Then, a little away from the phone, she added, "Maybe it's time to think about a retirement center for Louise."

"Mom, no. She doesn't need that." Sophie stood and started pacing. "She's fine, except for a sprained ankle. I shouldn't have told you. That's probably why Grandma didn't."

"Nonsense," Dad said in a soothing tone. "I'll talk to my mother. We won't do anything she doesn't want."

Sophie took a calming breath. "Anyway, I'm staying here for Christmas." Silence met her announcement. Had the line dropped? "Hello?"

"Well, if you'd rather spend the holiday with your grandmother than your parents, I guess there's nothing we can do about it," her mother huffed.

Sophie grimaced. "Mom, I'll come to California as soon as I can." If she could swing by to see them on the way to Zurich she would, but she couldn't make that promise. "It might not be until after my next job. We can go to your favorite spot for lunch." Which was a trendy restaurant in West Hollywood where people went to be seen.

"Please give my mother our love," Dad said. "We'll talk with you on Christmas Day." The phone clicked off.

Sophie held the phone away from her ear and stared at the device. They never failed to make her feel guilty and unimportant at the same time.

Would Mom or Dad tell the guys about Grandma? Sophie decided to call her eldest brother, Craig.

"Hey, little sis." Craig's booming voice made Sophie smile. "Are you in town?"

"No, I'm at Grandma's." She explained the situation.

"A puppy?" Craig whistled. "Riggs sounds more like a horse."

Sophie laughed. "He is big, that's for sure. I'm calling to see if you would talk to Dean and Sean about coming to visit Grandma soon." She could hear Craig's wife and kids in the background.

"Of course. Look, I have to go. We're heading out to do some Christmas shopping."

"Okay." She tried not to let her disappointment show in her voice. "Thank you. Love you, biggest brother," Sophie said.

Craig laughed. "Love you, too, little sis."

This time when she clicked off, she smiled. Her brothers had turned out pretty well. She hoped they thought the same of her.

CHAPTER
6

ednesday morning, David dressed to go into the office. He wore a custom-tailored gray pinstripe suit, white dress shirt, and red tie. He'd shaved and tamed his hair. The suit made him feel powerful, respectable. He made sure his black Florsheims shined.

He stepped into Troy's room. The boy slept curled in a ball on his side in the narrow twin-size bed. Toys and books were piled in the corner. They'd attempted to straighten up last night when they'd returned from having dinner with the ladies next door. Sophie was coming over to watch Troy while David took his meetings.

He could not express how relieved he was not to have to worry about Troy over the next few days. During today's meeting David would be negotiating a deal with the representatives of a large bank to take over their software needs. He needed to be focused and attentive. And thanks to Sophie, he would be.

Sitting on the edge of the bed, he put a hand on Troy's shoulder. "Hey, buddy. Time to wake up. Sophie will be here soon."

Troy stirred and burrowed deeper into the covers.

Undeterred, David tugged the comforter down. "Troy. We talked about this last night. You're going to spend a few hours with Sophie and Louise today. So you need to get up and get dressed so you're ready when she arrives."

Troy rolled to his back and stretched. "Why are you all fancy?"

"I'm going to the office, remember?"

Nodding, Troy sat up and yawned. David stood and went to the six-drawer dresser, where he took out a set of clean clothes. He laid them on the foot of the bed. "While you dress, I'll get breakfast ready."

Troy hopped out of the bed. His hair was mussed and standing up in places. His superhero footie pj's were a bit too big and hung on his slim frame. He looked so much like Daniel. A wave of grief hit David, and he had to steel himself. He couldn't let Troy see. He knelt down and gave Troy a hug. "I love you, buddy."

"I love you, Uncle David."

Regret lay heavy on David's heart for the distance that had grown between him and Daniel the past few years, but with Troy he had a second chance to do right by his brother.

In the kitchen, David put two blueberry waffles in the toaster. He poured orange juice into a plastic cup and set it at Troy's spot at the dining table.

The doorbell rang. Sophie was here.

David was surprised by the blast of anticipation that hit his chest. He opened the front door and smiled at the woman on the other side. Sophie's hair was down, with the sides clipped back by small silver barrettes. She had on jeans that hugged her curves and a deep blue sweater that reflected in the brightness of her eyes. Her warm smile twisted his chest up into knots. She was so pretty. He could stand there all day and be content to look at her.

"Good morning," she said.

Giving himself a mental shake, he stepped back so she could enter. "Good morning. How are you today?"

"I'm doing well. Grandma is sleeping in," she remarked with a laugh. "Too many rounds of UNO."

He chuckled. They'd played several hands of the card game last night after dinner. "I hadn't realized how competitive I could be. And Troy, too. Apparently it's a Murphy trait."

"It was fun to watch," she said. "I think in your business being competitive is a plus."

He conceded her words with a nod. "It has helped." He moved to the hallway. "Troy, Sophie's here." He turned back to the lovely lady standing by the dining room table. "I sure do appreciate you doing this for us."

She waved a hand. "It's my pleasure."

The sound of the toaster drew her attention. "I'll butter those for you."

"They're for Troy. Plates are in the cupboard above the toaster and utensils are in the drawer by the sink."

She nodded as she set about the task. "Does Troy have a car seat?"

"Yes. I'll set it inside the garage door before I leave."

She placed the plate with the buttered waffles on the table and moved gracefully toward him. "We're set here. Go on. Do what you need to do."

He hesitated. "You have my number, right? In case you need anything."

"I have both your cell and the office number."

"Okay. I'll be back by one."

"Great. If we're not here, we'll be next door."

Troy raced down the hall and skidded to a stop. "Hi, Sophie."

David dropped his chin at what Troy was wearing. He'd disregarded the jeans and long-sleeved shirt David had set out for him and instead wore a pair of red and white basketball shorts and a green-and-black-striped button-down shirt. His feet were bare but at least he'd combed his hair.

"My, don't you look good," Sophie exclaimed, trying to suppress a smile.

Troy grinned and wrapped his arms around her legs. She placed a hand on his back and met David's gaze.

He grimaced and shrugged. "There are jeans and a thermal shirt on his bed."

She grinned. "No worries. We'll figure it out. Now, go before you're late to your meeting."

With a salute, he hurried from the house, but he felt as if he'd left a little bit of his heart at her feet.

❄   ❄   ❄

David returned home shortly after one in the afternoon, his mood buoyant. The meeting with the bank had gone extremely well. The bank executive had promised to have a signed contract back to David right after Christmas. He couldn't believe how gratifying it was to know the company he'd built from the ground up was garnering such prestigious attention.

He parked his truck in the garage, noting the car seat was not where he'd left it. He entered the house and listened. All was quiet.

"Sophie?" he called out in a hushed whisper in case she'd somehow managed to convince Troy to take a nap.

There was no answer. And David was oddly disappointed.

He headed down the hall to his room, pausing briefly at the door to Troy's room. The bed was made and his toys more neatly arranged than they'd been this morning. A smile tugged at the corner of his mouth.

He proceeded to his own room and changed out of his suit into comfortable jeans, a thermal shirt similar to the one he'd laid out for Troy this morning, and tennis shoes. After carefully hanging up his suit, he walked to the kitchen for a glass of orange juice and stopped abruptly.

Not only was the kitchen spotless, but the living room had been cleared of the clutter and vacuumed. He could see the grooves from the vacuum machine in the carpet leading up to a new large square toy chest that was pushed up against the wall near the television. Acid churned in his stomach. The coffee and slice of zucchini bread he'd eaten at the office suddenly felt like a weight in his gut.

A tented note on the dining room table drew his attention. He read the note left in Sophie's swirling handwriting. She and Troy were next door with Louise and Riggs, and David was to come on over when he was ready.

Shaking his head, he crumpled the note and stuffed it into his pocket, and then headed next door.

"Come in!" Louise called at his knock.

He stepped inside and was grateful for the warming temperature since he'd forgotten to grab a jacket. Thankfully the morning rain had abated.

"David, how was your meeting?" Louise asked. She stood at the kitchen counter with her foot propped up on the rung of a stool.

"Really good." He leaned against the counter. "Where's Sophie and Troy?"

"Took Riggs for a walk." She lifted her foot from the stool and hopped to her wheelchair.

David rushed to help her. "Should you be doing that? Standing, I mean."

"Oh, it's fine. I can't sit all the time."

He took a seat on the couch across from her.

"Is something bothering you?"

He rubbed his palms on his thighs. She was perceptive. Or else he was transparent. "Sophie cleaned the house. She even bought a toy chest."

Louise's eyebrows rose. The expression so much like Sophie's he could only stare.

"And that's a problem because . . . ?" she prompted.

"Not a problem exactly. It wasn't part of our agreement." The weight of obligation pressed down on his chest.

"Oh. There was an agreement. Interesting. What exactly was in the agreement?"

He sighed. "It wasn't a formal thing." He rubbed the back of his neck, where tension tightened the muscles.

"Well, I'll leave it to you to discuss that with Sophie," Louise said. She cocked her head. "I think I hear them coming back now."

There was no mistaking Riggs's happy bark and Troy's squeal of delight or Sophie's lilting laughter. Eagerness to see Sophie rose within him. He tamped it down and instead focused on seeing Troy as the door opened. Riggs raced inside and headed straight to Louise for slobbery kisses. Troy came in next, looking so full of life. David's throat closed and he had to swallow to get the lump of emotion to go down. Troy stopped just inside the entryway and took off his shoes to carefully place them by the door.

David's mouth fell open with surprise, but he snapped his

mouth shut as Sophie entered and did exactly the same thing with her shoes.

"Uncle David!" Troy rushed to him in his socks. He wore the jeans and thermal shirt David had set out for him this morning.

David caught Troy in his arms and hugged him tight. He smelled clean and fresh like the outdoors. Troy's cold nose pressed against his neck. "Did you have a good time?"

He beamed, his eyes sparkling. "The best!"

David met Sophie's gaze. His heart did a little flip at the tender welcome he saw in her eyes.

She smiled. "How did it go today?"

"Well. Very well." Afraid she'd see the effect she had on him, he looked away to set Troy down. Then cleared his throat as he gathered his composure. He lifted his gaze back to Sophie. "Uh, can I talk to you in private?"

Her pretty eyes widened. "Sure."

"Troy, why don't you and I get a snack," Louise said, rolling into the kitchen. Troy happily followed her.

Knowing how easily conversations could be overheard in the house, David gestured toward the front door. Sophie nodded, stuck her feet back into her boots, and preceded him to the front porch. Before David could shut the door behind him, Riggs darted past him and out to the fenced front yard.

David ran a hand through his hair as he sought how to say what he needed to say. "Look, I appreciate that you're watching Troy. I can't express how grateful I am."

She leaned against the porch post. "We had fun."

He frowned and dove into what was bothering him. "You cleaned my house. You bought a toy chest."

She canted her head. "Yes."

"You didn't have to do that. I hadn't expected you to do house-keeping, too."

She shrugged off his concern. "I know. It was no big deal to do some cleaning."

It was to him. "I don't need a maid."

She frowned. "Troy helped me. It's important that Troy learn to pick up after himself and help out around the house." She shrugged, clearly puzzled. "I didn't think you'd mind the toy box. If you don't like it, I can take it back. I kept the receipt."

"It's not that I don't like it. I do. It's beautiful." Like her. He didn't like seeing the aggravated look in her eyes and hated worse knowing he'd put it there. But she didn't understand and he couldn't bring himself to explain.

"Did I overstep? I apologize."

Now she was apologizing and he should be the one groveling at her feet with gratitude. "No, you didn't overstep. It was very thoughtful. And you're right, I need to be more diligent about teaching Troy to take care of his things." He let out a dry laugh. "You must think I'm such a slob."

"Not at all," she replied in a cool tone.

"You're too kind." Kinder than he deserved. "I'll get Troy and we'll get out of your hair." He whistled and Riggs came running to his side. He petted Riggs behind the ear. "Wow, I wasn't sure if that would work."

"Who knew?" she quipped, but there was no smile to accompany her words. He'd hurt her feelings. Best to escape quickly before he totally blew it and alienated her altogether.

❄   ❄   ❄

Sophie's heart ached as she watched through the front window the Murphy boys head home. David was upset because she'd cleaned his house and worked with Troy on being disciplined to pick up after himself. She'd thought David would be pleased to come home to find the house neat. His response had stung.

She let out a frustrated huff. For a moment there, she'd thought they shared a connection. She'd seen the look of wonder and pure joy in David's eyes as he held Troy in his arms and hugged him close. And that look had spilled over to her, making her feel special and a part of their world.

The little family they were forming.

A bond she'd always secretly craved.

She should have known better.

She had to get a grip. She wasn't staying. There was no sense in growing close to either one of them. She'd only be setting herself up for heartbreak. No, thank you.

"Okay, spill it," Grandma said. She'd moved to her recliner and had taken the brace off her ankle so she could do the exercises the doctor had given her to do.

Taking a seat on the floor next to the recliner, Sophie made a face. "Men. I don't get them sometimes."

"The housecleaning?"

"He said something to you about it, too?"

"It wasn't part of your agreement."

Sophie let out a sigh. "Agreement. We didn't have an agreement." She picked at the carpet. "I don't know, Grandma. David confuses me. One minute I think we have this connection, and then the next he's pulling away."

"Maybe he's as scared as you are."

Her gaze snapped up. "What do you mean, 'scared'? I'm not scared of anything. I've traveled the world. I've gone into war zones and jungles and have dealt with wild animals and movie stars."

Grandma flexed her foot and extended it. "Yes, but when it comes to love, you tend to find the nearest exit." She chuckled.

"Excuse me? I'm not the one who bailed in my past relationships."

"You don't think flying off to foreign lands is a form of bailing?" Grandma arched an eyebrow. "You don't think turning down a proposal is a form of bailing?"

Sophie grimaced. She had confided in Grandma about her failed relationships. *"You are too flighty,"* Jason had said when she wouldn't move in with him. The label didn't sit well with her. She took her responsibilities seriously.

"You are commitment-shy," Andrew had claimed when she'd turned down his proposal.

He'd wanted her to give up her career. The one commitment she didn't have a problem making.

She knew they weren't right. But she also knew she needed to be careful.

She blew out another frustrated huff. "You sound like Mom."

Maybe Grandma and Mom were both right. Maybe subconsciously she hadn't wanted those relationships to last.

"Well, she was smart enough to marry your father, so I'll take that as a compliment." Grandma rolled her ankle slowly in circles. "Give David a break. This is all new to him."

"Allowing someone to do something nice for him is new to him?"

Grandma made a face. "I don't know about that. Though it might be something you'll want to ask him. But I would imagine suddenly having to be a father figure while running a company must be very stressful."

"Yes. It's all sorts of change at once. He's working on a really neat app for smartphones that could change people's lives."

"You sound impressed."

"I am." More than impressed. Attracted, too. A flutter of anxiety hit her and she put a hand on her tummy.

Grandma pinned her with a knowing look. "You like him."

"Sure." She narrowed her gaze. "But *like* is a far cry from *love*, Grandma."

"But it's a start."

No, it wasn't. Sophie wouldn't let it be. She wasn't going to fall in love with David. She wasn't staying here.

But she couldn't shake the nagging feeling that she'd miss them all. Especially a certain enigmatic man who made her pulse pound and put a yearning in her heart that she couldn't accept.

CHAPTER 7

David sat at his desk deep into coding his app. The house was dark except for the dining room light. Rain splattered the windows. The heater had kicked on a little while ago to chase away the chilly air. Snow was predicted for Christmas. David wasn't optimistic about the chances of that. This part of the state of Washington rarely saw the white stuff, but it wasn't totally unheard of, just unlikely.

Troy had fallen asleep a few hours earlier. Though exhausted from his day with Sophie and Riggs, he'd been full of stories about Riggs's antics and Sophie and all the fun they'd had together. Troy thought the world of Sophie.

David didn't blame him. She was pretty special. Troy had been so proud about helping Sophie clean house that guilt crept up David's spine.

He'd settle up with Sophie on Friday. He'd cut her a check for her time and then he'd feel better. A nagging voice scratched at his consciousness, saying Sophie might not be pleased. He shoved the thought aside. But wasn't able to put away the unease itching at him. He'd have to apologize to her. Again.

He shook his head, trying to stay focused on his work. But Sophie crept into his thoughts every few minutes.

He blew out a frustrated breath and got up to get a cup of coffee.

A soft knock at the front door stopped him in his tracks. He glanced at the clock on the wall. It was nearly midnight. Who would be knocking at this hour?

He opened the front door to find Sophie standing on the other side, looking drenched from the pouring rain. She was wearing a hooded rain slicker that cast a shadow over her face. Her shoulders were hunched and her arms clutched at her stomach. Concern chomped through him. "Sophie? Is everything okay?"

"Yes. Grandma and I and Riggs are fine. Sorry, didn't mean to scare you. I saw the light on and figured you were still up," she said with clattering teeth.

He needed to get her inside and out of the cold fast. "Come in before you freeze." He stepped back and she entered. If everything was okay, why was she here?

She shivered as he helped her out of the wet rain slicker. Beneath the slicker she had a silver laptop pressed to her chest. "I was hoping you'd be able to help me. I was uploading my photos from Gran Canaria and my computer wigged out."

He led her to the dining room table and took the laptop from her shaking hands. "Here, let me get you a cup of hot coffee or tea. Or hot cocoa. Troy loves hot cocoa."

"Do you have any herbal tea?" She followed him into the

kitchen. "I don't want the caffeine this late in the night." She eyed the half-full pot of coffee in the coffeemaker. "Apparently you do."

"Hey, if I'm going to get any work done while the little man sleeps, I need the jolt of energy." He set a tea kettle to boil and pulled out a tin of gourmet teas. "I think there's something herbal here. Daniel and Beth sent it to me in one of those gift baskets for Christmas a few years ago."

"It's a nice gift." She sorted through the teas until she found one she liked.

"I didn't appreciate Daniel and Beth the way I should have." He handed her a mug.

"I'm sure they knew you loved them."

He'd liked to think so, but he hadn't expressed the way he'd felt very often. He was determined not to make that mistake with Troy.

He hopped up at the first hint of whistle from the tea kettle, and he grabbed it and poured hot water over the tea bag. He got his coffee. As they went back to the dining room, he asked, "So what wigged out?"

"The screen. It did this funny squiggly thing, then died. It turned right back on but now I'm scared."

"Do you have everything backed up?"

"Yes. To the cloud, to a thumb drive, and to an external hard drive."

He laughed. "Okay. That's a bit of overkill but at least you don't have to worry about losing anything."

"I can't afford to lose anything."

Spoken like a person who'd had her value questioned. He certainly could appreciate the feeling. He opened the laptop and ran a diagnostic on the software. "This will tell us if it's a software problem, but it sounds more like a hard drive issue. Maybe a connection came loose in your travels."

When the diagnostic finished, he nodded at the results. "Yeah, you'll need to take this to the computer store. They'll open it up and check it out."

"I can't use it until then?"

"You can. As long as it continues to back up, you'll be fine."

"Okay. Thanks. I was freaking out and thought you'd know what to do." She closed the laptop lid.

"Can I see your pictures?"

She paused. "Sure. Do you want to see my official portfolio?" She reopened the laptop. Her fingers flew over the keyboard.

"Let's start with that. But I'd also like to see the ones that you hadn't planned to show the public."

She stared at him for a moment. "I don't usually show those to anyone but my agent."

She had the prettiest blue eyes. Sparkly, like gemstones. "There's a first time for everything."

"As long as you know that it takes a lot of shots to get a great one."

"I will find them all fascinating, I'm sure." He pulled two dining room chairs together and sat down.

She was slower to sit. He could see there was some sort of turmoil going on inside her. Her gaze was troubled. She bit her lip.

"Relax," he said. "I'm really interested." And he was. She saw things in such a unique way. Surely that extended to her photography. He wanted to see what she saw through the lens of her camera.

"Okay, we'll start with the official portfolio, though." She brought up a beautifully designed site, featuring photos broken into categories such as people and places, commercial, fashion, and animals. They clicked through the pictures, starting with people. There were celebrities, brides and grooms. Portraits of interesting faces. Landscapes that took his breath away.

She'd gone to so many places he'd only read about—jungles, island paradises, and deserts. The commercial tab was full of advertising-type pictures, a few of which he recognized. He was impressed, not only by her talent but also by the breadth of her work.

The fashion images showed runway models strutting down the catwalk and outdoor scenes, both urban and country, with beautiful women and men wearing designer clothing.

But it was the images of animals that grabbed his attention. A python in India, coiled and ready to strike. A burro along the razor-thin edge of a cliff in South America. A humpback whale balancing on its tail in the ocean.

"Those are fabulous." He couldn't keep the awe from his voice. "Your family must be so proud of you." He was proud of her and he'd only just met her. To be so accomplished at such a young age. And the awards some of her photos had garnered were top-notch.

She made a dismissive noise. "I doubt my family has taken the time to look at my work."

Surprise flashed through him. He knew how proud Louise was of her granddaughter. "What? How can that be?"

"My parents indulged my photography, but my mom wanted me to follow in her footsteps and go into show business. Dad, well, he always compliments my pictures but he gushes over my brothers. Grandma's the only one who's been supportive of me."

"Louise gave you your first camera, right?"

"Yes. It was her way of giving me something to do because my brothers wouldn't let me tag along with them." She gave a rueful shake of her head. "I'm sorry. I don't mean to rag on my family. They're great in their way."

"But you don't feel like your parents and siblings take your work seriously."

Her eyes widened. "Exactly. Little Sophie and her camera."

He brushed back a lock of hair that had fallen over her cheek. "I like Sophie and her camera."

Had he really just said that? By the stunned look in her eyes, yes he had. And he did. He liked her. And owed her an apology. "Hey, I apologize for overreacting about you cleaning my house."

She dropped her gaze. "Why did you?"

That was a loaded question and one he wasn't ready to answer. "I didn't want you to think that was why I agreed to you helping me out with Troy." He shrugged. "Plus I was a bit embarrassed by how messy we are, er, were."

Her lips curved upward, drawing his gaze. "No need to be embarrassed."

He lifted his gaze and locked eyes with her. The yearning he saw there reached out to wrap around him. He forced himself to focus his attention back onto the laptop. Best to keep things between them on a friendly, platonic level. "How about showing me the pictures that didn't make it onto your website now?"

"Okay." She clicked through to another file.

For an hour they looked through photos of exotic, far-off landscapes, glamorous people, and heartbreaking conditions in Third World countries. Several shots were of her with a different child in a different part of the world. "Who took these?"

"I set a timer."

Another image rose of Sophie sitting atop a very large elephant. "Whoa. Where was this taken?"

"Thailand," she said with such wistfulness, he guessed she missed being there.

How tame life here in the Pacific Northwest must seem to her. How boring he must seem. He could never compete with the life she led. Not that he intended to compete. But seeing the reality of her exciting and fast-paced world was reason enough to keep his heart firmly locked behind the walls he'd built over the years.

It didn't matter if he was attracted to Sophie and liked her a lot. He couldn't let her into his heart. He couldn't let his defenses down. Not now, not ever.

❄   ❄   ❄

Thursday afternoon, David sat in a meeting with a team of people from an advertising agency that wanted his company to do an overhaul of their software programs to up the company's efficiency. As David's chief financial officer, Ken Larson, and the ad agency's CFO talked dollars, David's mind wandered to Sophie.

When she'd arrived this morning, she'd looked so fresh and pretty in jeans and a green sweater that deepened the color of her eyes to match the inviting waters surrounding the islands in her photographs.

He'd been hard-pressed to leave. But leave he did. Being around Sophie wasn't good for him.

He hadn't been able to fall asleep after she'd left his house last night. His mind had wanted to play "what if?" What if he and Sophie fell in love? What if Sophie were content to live in Bellevue and help him raise Troy?

What if he and Troy went with her on her travels? What if he developed his app and could afford to hire someone else to run his company so he could spend all his time with Troy and Sophie?

But he'd learned as a kid that what-ifs were fantasies that never happen. And letting his mind entertain such ridiculous thoughts wasn't productive. And being productive was the key to success.

"We're in agreement, then," David heard his CFO say, bringing him back to the moment. Both men turned their attention to their employers. David trusted Ken with the numbers and gave a nod of consent.

"Yes," the ad agency owner said. "Mr. Murphy, how quickly will we be able to implement the new software?"

Looking at his notes, he said, "By March."

"Wonderful. I look forward to that day."

They shook hands, and David walked the man to the door. "We appreciate you taking a chance on us."

"Your company has an excellent reputation, Mr. Murphy."

"We do our best," David replied, pleased by the encouraging words. He and his team had worked hard to get where they were. In an area with more than three hundred software and tech companies competing for business, David's start-up was gaining traction. To know that others thought well of the company meant a lot to him.

After the client left, David wrapped up a few other issues with his design team and his production team before heading home. He parked in the garage and entered the quiet, empty house. For reasons he couldn't explain, he was anxious to see Sophie. Troy, he amended. He was anxious to see his nephew. He hurried to the Griffiths' without changing clothes.

Louise answered the door. She had a set of crutches under her arms. "Welcome to the North Pole."

Louise's living room did indeed look like a toy factory, complete with a little elf wearing a Santa hat and a large dog posing as a reindeer. Troy sat on the floor with a tape dispenser in his hands and carefully measured off a piece to hand to Sophie. She sat beside him with a matching Santa hat perched on her bent head. She took the piece of tape and put it on a festively wrapped present in her lap. There were stacks of wrapped gifts alongside a stack of unwrapped toys.

"What is all of this?" David asked.

"Toys for the needy," Troy announced proudly.

David's breath seized in his chest. Old memories rushed to the forefront of his mind. Memories of Christmases when he and Daniel were young and a parade of nice people would stop by with prettily wrapped presents to give to the poor little Murphy children. The shame and humiliation of knowing the community pitied them. He could still hear the schoolyard taunts. He shuddered.

"David? Are you okay?"

Sophie's concerned voice broke through the haze that had come over him.

"Maybe you should sit down," she suggested. "You look a little green."

He did feel as if he might throw up. He sank onto the couch. "You bought a lot of things."

"I picked the toys out," Troy told him with solemn eyes. "They are for kids that don't have homes or as many toys as I do."

David wanted to smile at his nephew's exuberance but his mouth wouldn't work. His face felt frozen. He settled for a nod.

"Troy even offered to give away a few of his own toys," Sophie said with a pleased smile at Troy.

David grit his teeth together as bile roiled in his stomach. Feeling Sophie's assessing gaze, he stayed focused on Troy. "That's very generous, Troy."

The little boy nodded. "My daddy always said that we give to others because God gave us so much."

David's heart spasmed. Daniel, the eternal optimist. "Your daddy was a smart man," he managed to say around the lump in his throat. "You're just like him."

Troy grinned.

Sophie rose to place the gift on the pile. "That's enough for tonight. We'll finish this tomorrow and drop them off at the church." She held out her hand to Troy. He set the tape aside and grasped her hand. She hefted him to his feet. "Good job today, kiddo. I sure appreciate your help."

"I like helping." Troy put his hands on his hips and surveyed the toys. "I might need to come over sooner tomorrow than after lunch."

"You can come over any time you want," Sophie said and took him by the shoulders and turned him around. "Why don't you put on your coat now?"

Troy didn't argue. He just ran to where his coat hung on a rack by the front door. Riggs jumped up and chased after, clearly thinking they were playing.

David stood, meeting Sophie's curious regard. "You're good with him."

She flashed him a smile. "He's a great kid."

Taking a bracing breath, David nodded. "Daniel and Beth would be very proud of him." He held Sophie's gaze a moment longer. Such pretty eyes. She made him want to open up, to think that maybe she'd understand. But he couldn't. And he didn't want to see the pity in her eyes when she learned of his background. He broke eye contact and headed for Troy. "We'll see you tomorrow."

She followed him to the door and laid a hand on his arm before he stepped outside. "Are you okay?"

"Of course." The words were stiff against his tongue.

"If you want to bring Troy over around ten tomorrow morning, he can have lunch with us."

Her generosity touched him. "Are you sure?"

"Yes."

He covered her hand with his. Her hand was warm and soft and it took everything in him not to pull her closer. "Thank you. I'm sure he'd like that." He let go and ushered Troy home before he gave in to the attraction tugging at him.

❄   ❄   ❄

After dinner and a bath, David sat on Troy's bed with Troy leaning against his side, his small head resting against his chest. Though David hated to let go of the moment, he closed the fifteenth book he'd read and said, "Okay, buddy. That's it for tonight. I'm storied out."

A sleepy Troy scooted down beneath the covers and laid his head on the pillow. "Will you pray? My daddy used to pray with me at bedtime."

David's heart squeezed tight. This was the first time Troy had made this request. David should have thought of it. Of course Daniel had prayed. He'd always been faithful to God, even when life was spinning out of control.

David's faith was more hit or miss. He slid to his knees beside the bed and folded Troy's tiny hands in his. "Dear Lord, thank you for this day. Thank you for our new friends, Louise and Sophie. Thank you for Troy. Please watch over us as we sleep and as we go about our days. Amen."

Troy tightened his hold on David's hand. "Sophie's pretty, isn't she, Uncle David?"

Biting back a smile in the face of Troy's solemn eyes, David nodded. "Yes. Very pretty."

"Do you like her?"

Wary of where this was going, he replied, "Yes. She's a very nice lady."

Troy nodded, seeming satisfied with the answer.

"Troy, Sophie's only in town for a short time to visit her grandma," he said, needing to make sure his nephew understood that Sophie wasn't a permanent fixture in their lives. "She'll be leaving soon."

"Leaving? Where will she go?"

"Far away."

Troy's lip poked out. "Oh. Why?"

"Her job takes her all over the world."

Troy seemed to be digesting the information. Then he asked, "Your job won't take you all over the world, will it?"

"No. And if it did I'd take you with me." He kissed Troy on the forehead. "Good night, buddy."

Troy rolled to his side. "Good night. Sleep well. I love you, Uncle David."

Tenderness filled his chest. "I love you too, buddy."

Oh, Daniel. We miss you so much. David had let a singular focus on work keep him from Daniel for too long and now he was gone. But Daniel's legacy lived on in Troy.

With a heavy heart, David left Troy's room and headed back to his makeshift desk at the dining room table. He hoped to get some work done before Troy had a nightmare and required his attention. Before he could delve into the work and lose himself, his cell phone buzzed with an incoming text. Sophie. Asking if he was up. She was outside his house and wanted to talk.

His pulse sped up. He wanted to see her. Needed to see her for reasons he didn't fully understand. And that scared him more than he wanted to admit.

CHAPTER 8

Sophie tightened her hold on Riggs's leash. He sniffed the bushes around David's porch while she waited to see if David would respond to her text. She stomped her feet softly to keep warm. A chill seeped through her raincoat. She wasn't sure what madness had prompted her to send the text in the first place. It was obvious something had been bothering David today when he'd arrived at Grandma's to pick up Troy.

She hoped she hadn't overstepped again. She hadn't touched his house today, but she hadn't needed to. They'd kept it tidy. She was so proud of Troy for returning his toys to his new chest like they'd talked about.

She was surprised and a bit wary by the amount of pride she felt, because she wasn't parent material. She was wandering into dangerous territory here. Everything she'd suggested had been tricks and tips she'd learned from the parade of nannies who'd come and gone from her life.

The shopping trip with Troy had been a pleasant experience, which surprised her. Not that she'd expected it to be a disaster, but she hadn't thought it would go so smoothly. She'd been afraid he'd want her to buy him things when the purpose of the trip had been to find gifts for underprivileged children.

He'd seemed to understand and been very thoughtful in picking toys and warm clothing items for both girls and boys between the ages of two and ten. He'd really considered each present and never once asked for something for himself. Though she did manage to slip in a couple of superhero action figures that he'd said were his favorites without him seeing.

She'd been so happy with his behavior she'd offered to buy him candy as they were checking out and he'd picked out a kind he'd said his uncle liked. Such a thoughtful kid.

She wished she'd known his parents. They'd done a good job in such a short time of instilling compassion and generosity into their son.

When she and Troy returned with their bounty, they'd spent the rest of the time at Grandma's. She was almost sad that tomorrow would be the last day she'd have alone with Troy since David was taking the rest of the next two weeks off.

Sad because she was going to miss hanging out with Troy. He was such a delight. Yes, he could be a bit of a handful, testing boundaries and struggling with self-control, but he was also a good kid with a good heart.

And she'd miss seeing David dressed for the office. She had to admit he'd looked handsome in his suit. She'd liked the gray suit yesterday. But today he'd had on a navy pinstripe with a light-blue button-down shirt and red-and-navy-striped tie that had made him look powerful and confident. She wondered if he wore a suit every day he went into the office or just the days when he had meetings. He was such an interesting man. Charming and friendly at times, then stoic, almost brooding. It was confusing and intriguing at once.

But she didn't need the confusion in her life. And she refused to allow the intriguing notion to take root. Her goal was to get Grandma on her feet again and then take off. She had a really exciting job lined up. One that could set her up for a long time. She needed to keep her focus on the future.

A shiver worked its way over her. The weather was chilly, but thankfully wasn't raining right now. The neighborhood was quiet, but festive with twinkling lights on the houses. Except for David's. He hadn't put up lights. She wondered why. He'd so generously put up Grandma's lights, why not hang any on his own house? Maybe he would over the weekend.

As the seconds ticked by, she debated walking away. She could talk to David tomorrow or Saturday, when they went Christmas tree shopping. She'd almost forgotten about the planned excursion. Yes, she should wait until then instead of standing here on his porch like a stalker. She turned to go as David's front door swung wide and he walked out onto the porch. He pulled the door but left a slight crack, no doubt in case Troy called out to him.

The warm, yellow glow of the porch light revealed the bright shine in his gray eyes. He'd changed into jeans and a pullover hoodie. A five o'clock shadow darkened his jawline. He looked different from the professional man from earlier, but just as powerfully handsome. A quiver of attraction shot through her.

She inhaled deeply, catching a whiff of his cologne, a musky masculine scent that made her want to nuzzle close to him. She stayed rooted to the porch at arm's distance away. Safer that way. For her piece of mind.

"Hey," he said and bent to rub Riggs behind the ears.

Was his greeting directed at her or the dog? She found herself tongue-tied as she watched him giving the puppy so much affection. She wanted to be on the receiving end of that affection. Her pulse raced.

She'd made a mistake by asking him to come out. Drawing him onto the porch where it was just the two of them sent longing winding through her. She should have just kept on walking and let things stay the way they were. But she wasn't one to ignore her curiosity. He'd been upset, and if she'd done something to offend, she needed it brought to light so she could apologize and they could move on.

David straightened. "It's a nice night for a walk."

"It is." She fiddled with the leash, working up the nerve to broach the subject of his obvious upset. "Hey, so, I had the distinct impression you were bothered by something when you picked up Troy today. Did I do anything to offend you again?"

He groaned. "No. Of course not. It isn't you. It's me."

"That sounds like a breakup line."

His eyes widened. "I'm not—I mean, what?"

"Nothing," she mumbled, embarrassed by her choice of words. They weren't dating, so he couldn't break up with her. Though the idea of dating David latched onto her mind.

What would it be like to spend time alone with him, away from kids, dogs, and grandmas?

She gave herself a mental shake. Not going to happen. Dating wasn't on her agenda while in Washington. She was leaving to further her career, and nothing was going to stand in the way. Certainly not a man. No matter how handsome or how much he made her heart flutter. "So what's going on? I promise, I'm a good listener."

"I'm sure you are." He jammed his hands into his pockets. Riggs lay down, putting his paws on David's foot. They shared a smile.

"I really appreciate how well you're taking care of Troy," David said. "He's become very fond of you and Louise. It's great for him to have stability after suffering so much loss."

His words slipped between her ribs with swift and lethal accuracy. They both knew she was leaving and what it would do to Troy when she did. Her stomach roiled. "We're fond of him, too."

"When do you leave again?"

The pointed question lanced her heart. She sighed. "I've told you. After New Year's."

"Right."

He still hadn't answered her question. She debated letting it go. She had no reason to pry, especially if she wanted to keep from becoming too attached, too involved with him.

But there was something about David that called to her. Something that made her believe he carried a heavy burden beyond the obvious one of sudden parenthood and a growing company. And she wanted to know what it was, and despite knowing she shouldn't, she wanted to help. Her brothers would say she was meddling.

She could almost see her middle brother, Dean, wagging a finger at her, saying, *"Sis, you think you're helping but you're only making things worse with your meddling. Stay out of other people's business."* Meaning *his* business. Though her other two brothers shared the sentiment.

What would David think? Would he resent her for offering her support? Only one way to find out. "You can talk to me. I won't judge."

✻ ✻ ✻

David studied the pretty lady standing on his porch. Though the wall sconce created shadows that played across her face, he could see her earnest expression. Her blue eyes held his gaze. She had such a good heart. A giving heart. She wanted him to talk to her about what had him upset this afternoon. But he had a feeling her request came because she saw him as a project. Someone who needed to be fixed. How many times had others stepped into his life with the same agenda? Too many for him to count.

He didn't take handouts, nor did he want to be anyone's good deed. Not even a beautiful and compassionate woman such as Sophie. "You won't judge, huh?"

"No, I won't."

"Good to know."

Her eyebrows pinched together. "Did something happen at your office?"

She was tenacious, he'd give her that. "No. Everything there is going well. My staff is prepared for me to take some time off." He grinned. "In fact, we're closing the office on the twenty-third."

Her influence on him. While he'd been making plans to take time away from the office, it had occurred to him that very few of his employees had taken vacation days. A few sick days here and there, but his staff was loyal and hardworking. And they deserved a reward for their dedication. "I figured we could all use a few days away from work. Paid, of course."

A smile broke out across her face. "That's very generous of you."

Her praise puffed up his chest a bit. He'd known she'd like that. Though he wasn't sure why her approval meant so much to him. Crazy. She was only temporarily in his and Troy's life.

Which was something he really needed to make sure Troy understood. He'd already told Troy that Sophie would be leaving after Christmas, but he had a feeling the child would need to be reminded often so his heart didn't break when the time came for Sophie to say good-bye.

She narrowed her gaze a bit. He could see her mind working. "So if work isn't bothering you, then what?"

Like a dog with a bone. He would admire her stubbornness if it weren't directed at him. "Are you always so relentless?"

She shrugged with a wry grimace. "According to my brothers, yes."

He wondered what made her tick. What kind of sister was she? What kind of girlfriend would she be? Strike that. He wasn't interested in a girlfriend. He was so overwhelmed as it was by life, adding a relationship to the mix would only complicate things. But he couldn't deny he would like to know more about her. It couldn't hurt to fill in some details as long as he kept his heart from falling for her. Besides, if he could direct the conversation away from himself, all the better. "How many brothers do you have?"

"Three."

That surprised him. She'd said her parents were workaholics. He'd expected her to be an only child or have one sibling at the most. "Where do you fit in?"

"They are all older. Craig is thirty-five and a doctor, married to Leann, whom I adore. They have two kids, Michael and Gregory. Then there's Dean. He's thirty-two, a lawyer, married to Caitlyn, and they have a newborn girl named Deidra, after Cait's mother. And Sean's thirty, a pharmacist, and recently married to Rhonda."

He couldn't help the stab of envy at the large family she enjoyed. "You're the lone holdout, huh?"

"Yes." She blew out a breath. "Much to my mother's dismay."

"Why's that?"

"That my mom's dismayed? She thinks if I don't get married by the time I'm thirty then I won't." She shook her head. "I'm twenty-eight. There's still time."

"If thirty is the cutoff to be married, I'm doomed. Thirty was three years ago." Not that marriage was on his mind.

"There's no time limit on getting married. That's just my mother's weirdness."

He chuckled. "Do you want to get married someday?"

She shrugged again. "I'm not sure. I don't have a stellar track record when it comes to relationships."

He could relate. "Too career-oriented?"

She frowned. "Why would you say that?"

"You travel for your work, live in a studio apartment that you admit is more of a storage and staging place than a home. You seem perfectly happy unattached and unfettered."

Her eyes widened. Apparently he'd hit the mark with his observations. "What about you? Is marriage in your plans?"

"Definitely too work-oriented. My company comes first."

"But you have Troy now," she gently reminded him. "He should come before work."

There was that. A game changer. "Yes. So now I have two priorities. I don't think I could handle juggling a third one."

She looked away. What did it matter to her that he didn't have room in his life for marriage? She wasn't searching for a soul mate either.

When she glanced back at him there was determination in her blue eyes. "You still haven't answered my question. Why were you upset this afternoon?"

He barked out a shallow laugh. "You're not going to let that go, are you?"

Her chin lifted. "No." Riggs must have sensed the change in her demeanor because he rose and nudged her with his nose. She reached down to stroke his head. David watched the way the dog's eyes rolled back in pure joy. The yearning to have Sophie running her fingers through his own hair made his scalp itch.

Snapping his mind away from the dog's obvious pleasure, David debated hedging. He really didn't want to go down this road with her, but had a feeling she'd just keep pressing until he broke. Better to just get it over with. To put it out there and see how fast she ran. "Seeing all those gifts and hearing Troy talk about the needy brought back memories from my childhood."

She cocked her head. "Did you and your family give to the poor?"

Acid burned in his gut. Such an innocent query. A valid one. Although everything inside of him wanted to walk away from her question, the answer slipped from his mouth anyway. "We *were* the poor."

She inhaled sharply. "Oh. I'm sorry. I didn't mean—"

No sense in letting her feel bad for asking. "It's okay. No need to apologize."

He wasn't sure why he'd told her. He'd never admitted the truth to anyone before. He'd kept that part of his life from the public, from his employees and his investors. From anyone in his life. No one needed to know he'd come from nothing. He didn't want anyone feeling sorry for him, or giving him a boost just because of his childhood circumstances.

But Sophie had a quality that made him want to tell her things he'd never told to anyone else. He steeled himself against the pity he expected to see in her eyes. "Daniel and I were on the receiving end of others' charity more often than I care to remember."

"Ah."

The tenderness in her eyes pricked him. No doubt her compassionate heart was flooded with sympathy. His fingers curled at his sides but he refrained from backing away from her. He'd started this by opening up and he'd take the hit. Better for her to learn now that he wasn't like her and therefore not someone she should ever get emotionally involved with. They were from opposite worlds.

She put a hand on his arm. "And receiving gifts from strangers made you feel dependent and out of control."

Her insight left him speechless. How could she know or possibly understand what he'd felt when her life had been so different? She'd never wanted for food or shelter. She'd never been teased or laughed at because she had on someone else's cast-off clothes, or had to stand in line at the welfare office for food stamps, bread, and milk.

Despite her parents' lack of attention, she'd had a privileged life. Still did.

He should turn around and go back inside his house and leave her to think what she wanted, but he couldn't make himself move.

"Your parents?"

"Did the best they could," he was quick to say. He didn't want her to think less of them. "They'd loved each other and their children above all else. My dad dropped out of high school to work on the family wheat farm. He and Mom were high school sweethearts, and when she finished high school, she married my dad and helped my grandparents. Daniel and I came along pretty quickly. Unfortunately, hard times hit."

His gut clenched at the thought of all his family had suffered. He had to force himself to continue. He'd come this far, he had to go all the way. "There were problems on the farm. Drought and then a diseased crop. Pressure from the bank."

Sophie made a distressed noise.

He had to look away to continue. "Dad and Granddad did everything they could but weren't able to save the farm. By the time I was four we lived in a small trailer on the edge of town. Dad did day labor for other farms in the area. Mom took a job at the convenience store." He couldn't keep the bitterness from creeping into his tone. "There's a superstore on our farmland now."

She squeezed his arm. "That must have been hard on your family."

Riggs shifted his attention to David. The pup moved to lean against David's leg. Reaching down, David uncurled his hand to bury his fingers in the dog's fluffy fur. "Heartbreaking was more like it."

The memories battered at him, bringing with them the anxiety and fear that had plagued him for so long. Obviously he hadn't buried his past as deeply as he'd thought he had. "My grandparents both died shortly afterward."

Were those tears in her eyes? "And your parents? Do they still live . . ."

"In Chewelah. No. They're gone. Mom died from the flu. We didn't have insurance, so she wouldn't go to the doctor, and the over-the-counter medication did nothing for her."

"That's so sad." Sophie's voice broke.

"We were sad. Dad's heart couldn't take it. He suffered a heart attack a few months later."

Her hand went to her throat. "I'm so sorry. How old were you?"

"A sophomore in high school. Daniel was already working for the post office by then and he was able to become my guardian even though he was only four years older."

Still young. Too young to take on raising a teenager. "I owe Daniel so much for everything he did for me."

"You've taken in his son," she said softly.

"Taking in Troy's a small price for the years Daniel had sacrificed for me," he said. "It was Daniel who made sure we had a roof over our heads and food to eat. It was Daniel who pushed me to get good grades and to apply for scholarships." Guilt swamped him for so many reasons. The sacrifices Daniel had made for him. The time lost between them. "He'd started out as a custodian at the post office and climbed his way up."

"He sounds like he was a great guy."

He nodded, wishing he'd told Daniel how much he'd appreciated all he'd done, but the drive to succeed had kept David silent. "He was a great guy. When I came west to go to college he followed, taking a job with the city of Bellevue as a carrier. He enjoyed delivering the mail."

"It's a noble profession."

"True. Daniel had such a bright outlook on life. He'd taken everything in stride, always believing things would work out. He took solace in his faith and his family, while I found security in my work. That drove us apart in the end." David's voice trembled. "I miss my brother."

Her arms slid around him. Stunned, he wrapped his arms around her. Her hair smelled like sunshine after a spring rain. He shouldn't enjoy having her in his embrace as much as he did. And he was helpless to do anything about it. Even if he wanted to.

CHAPTER
9

"N ow I understand," Sophie murmured against David's chest.

David struggled to comprehend her words. Despite the fact that they were standing on his porch in the cold, he only felt the warmth of holding her in his arms. "Understand what?"

"Why you have such trouble accepting help. Why you feel obligated to repay any kindness."

"I don't—" Even as he began to protest, he knew what she said was truth. But that was who he was, what made him who he was. He couldn't change.

She pulled back and looked into his face. "David, you can't let your past define who you are."

Whoa. He stepped back, letting his arms drop to his sides. "I don't let the past define me." A fire ignited deep inside him. "I'm who I am because I fought my way out. I studied hard and won scholarships. Nobody handed me anything."

"That's admirable, but it sounds lonely."

"I'm not lonely." The words rang hollow in the cold night air. He frowned, considering her words. "When I'm at work, I'm surrounded by my employees. And now I have Troy. That's all I need."

He didn't need anyone else. But looking into her eyes, an empty spot in his heart opened up like a wound. He'd be crazy to think she could fill it. Would want to fill it. She was leaving. She'd made her plan clear. Her life was on the move, wandering the world with her camera. Looking at life through her lens.

Settling down with a ready-made family wasn't something she wanted or needed. He'd be setting himself up for regret and heartache if he allowed himself to become too attached to this woman.

Or to let Troy become too used to having her in their lives. It was imperative that David talk more to Troy tomorrow about Sophie's temporary status in their lives. This was a nice break from reality for them both, but he didn't have it in him to fall for Sophie. Not now, while Troy needed him so much. David's priority had to be on his nephew and his company. There wasn't room for anyone else. Not even the lovely Sophie.

"Thank you for explaining. I understand how hard it was for you as a young boy." She visibly pulled herself together and moved toward the stairs. "Please don't begrudge Troy the opportunity to be blessed by giving to others."

He didn't like the note of censure in her tone. Or the self-reproach crawling up his throat. He'd been so busy shoring up his defenses against any storm that might hit, he hadn't taken the time to look outward. To give back to the community. A wave of shame washed over him. He jammed his hands into pockets. "I'm not. I wouldn't. I think it's a nice gesture."

"Only a gesture?" She considered him for a long moment. "It's more blessed to give than to receive," she said. "I never really understood that verse in Acts but now I think I do."

Sophie's words reverberated inside his head. A blessing to give? "I've never thought of giving in that way before."

"Kindness to others is an expression of faith in God." She tugged on Riggs's leash. "It's late. I should get back to Grandma."

Suddenly he didn't want her to go. He wanted to explore these new thoughts she'd planted inside his head. But the smart thing to do was let her return home so he could figure out his life on his own. Like always. But she'd given him plenty to chew on. "Good night, Sophie."

"I'll see you tomorrow." She and Riggs walked away.

He stood on the porch long after they'd gone inside Louise's house. His mind was mired in turmoil. Why had he told her about his childhood? Why did he feel so . . . empty?

A cry from inside jolted through him. He hurried to Troy's room. Light from the hallway slashed across Troy's bed.

"Daddy!" Troy sat up, his wild-eyed gaze unfocused as he sobbed.

David's heart pitched and he gathered Troy close to his chest. "Shhhh. It's okay. I've got you."

"Daddy?" Troy clutched at David's chest. Then his gaze cleared. "Uncle David." He threw his arms around his neck. "I had a scary dream."

"It was only a dream. You're safe here." He eased Troy back to the pillow and brushed aside a lock of hair that had fallen into his eyes. "How about if I lay down with you until you fall back to sleep."

Troy scooted over to make room.

David lay down next to his nephew, the narrow bed barely

holding his large frame. The boy curled into his side. Tenderness flooded David. Troy was his priority. His family. His to protect. From all of life's challenges. Including one gorgeous, generous photographer.

* * *

Sophie and Troy loaded the last few presents they'd finished wrapping today into the back of Sophie's rental car. It was nearly noon and a drizzle had started. Riggs trailed happily along behind them as they'd transferred the gifts from the house to the car.

David was due back after lunch, which meant they had an hour to drop off the packages at Grandma's church and get back before he returned from his office.

After hearing his story last night, she thought it best to deliver their packages while he was at work. She didn't want to dredge up any more horrible memories for him. Distress lay heavy within her for the traumatic and hard life he and his family had led. And were still leading, what with his brother and sister-in-law's tragic deaths.

Why were some people touched by heartache while others never experienced it?

She'd never gone through loss the way David and his family had. Sure, she resented the time her parents devoted to their careers rather than to her, and the way her older brothers had not liked having their younger sister dogging their every step. But that was petty and paltry compared to the suffering of the Murphy family.

She knew God never promised life would be fair. He'd only promised He'd be there for those who believed in Him, through the good and the bad. The knowledge didn't lessen the heartache but did make it bearable.

"Okay, kiddo, I think we're all set." She closed the back hatch. "Jump into your car seat."

She stood next to the car and held the door open as Troy scrambled into the backseat, where she'd secured his car seat. He strapped himself in and gave her the thumbs-up sign. He looked so cute she couldn't resist taking his picture.

She opened the front passenger side door to grab her camera where she'd tucked it on the floor. She snapped off several shots of Troy mugging for the camera. Riggs barked and jumped in the car.

"Oh no you don't, boy." She shooed him out.

"Come up here with me, Riggs," Grandma called from where she sat on the porch, out of the rain.

Sophie grabbed him by the collar. "You need to stay and keep Grams company."

Grandma had elected to stay behind while Sophie and Troy dropped off the gifts that would be distributed on Christmas Eve. Sophie led Riggs to the porch.

Grandma took ahold of his collar. "Have fun."

"We'll be back soon." Sophie kissed Grandma's cheek and then hurried to the driver's seat of the SUV, but before she could put the vehicle in reverse, David's truck pulled in behind her, blocking the driveway. What was he doing home so soon? She hoped nothing was wrong.

She hopped out and met him at the back end of her car. He popped open an umbrella and held it over them. She appreciated his thoughtfulness. He wore a black suit today, with a light green shirt and a coordinating tie. So handsome. The thrill of attraction flared bright, warming her from the inside out.

It didn't matter if he were dressed to impress or relaxed in jeans and unshaven, she could get used to seeing him in all his different versions of attire. Formal, casual . . . or muddy.

Giving herself a mental shake, she said, "You're home early. Is everything okay?"

"Yes." His gaze went to the cargo area of the SUV. His jaw worked. He rolled his shoulders and met her gaze. "I'd like to come with you and Troy when you drop off the presents. If that's okay?"

Delighted and confused by the request, she said, "Of course. We're going to the church. The gifts won't be distributed until Christmas Eve."

Relief crossed his face. "Give me five minutes to park and change clothes, okay?"

Puzzling over this turn of events, she nodded. "Sure."

He pushed the umbrella into her hands and then hurried back to his truck. While she waited for him, she opened Troy's door. "Your uncle's coming with us."

"Yay!" Troy's cheer gladdened her heart.

"Sophie?" Grandma called from the porch. No doubt she was curious about David's unscheduled return.

It was perplexing. Sophie had assumed from David's reaction yesterday that he wouldn't want anything to do with today's mission. What had changed his mind? Why the change of heart? Had her words last night affected him? If so, she was pleased. Either way she was proud of him, because she knew this would cost him emotionally.

Sophie closed Troy's door and went to Grandma. She'd confided in her about David's upbringing this morning over coffee. "David wants to come with us."

"Good for him," Grandma said. "That pleases me."

"Me, too." And it really did.

She was pleased he'd left work early to be a part of something that meant so much to Troy. And she couldn't help but be thrilled at spending a bit more time with both of the Murphy boys. Though there was nothing boyish about David.

He was 100 percent man and her female senses tingled with alertness every time he was near. It was a pleasant feeling—but definitely a dangerous one.

Just because she was attracted to him didn't mean she could let her heart get all mushy about him. That would only make it hurt when the time came to leave. It was going to be hard enough saying good-bye to Troy and Grandma as it was. But Sophie and Grandma would Skype and email like they usually did. Maybe she could send postcards to Troy.

"Invite David and Troy to dinner tonight," Grandma instructed. "I'd like Simon to meet David. I think that would be a good thing."

Sophie wouldn't mind having more company to offset the awkwardness of meeting the man interested in her grandmother. "I will," she assured Grandma. "Here he comes. We'll be back in an hour and then we can start cooking."

"I'll get things prepped while you're out."

They would be cooking all afternoon in preparation for the dinner with Simon. And Grandma had promised to show Sophie how to perfect the persimmon cookies recipe. "Don't do too much. I want to help."

"Then I'll go through my closet and decide what to wear tonight," Grandma declared.

"Something in blue to bring out your eyes," Sophie suggested.

Grandma grinned. "Quite right. Gotta play up the only asset I have left."

"Grams, that's not true," Sophie chided. "You're beautiful and intelligent and full of life. Any man worth his salt would be blessed to find himself in your company."

Grandma's face turned pink and her eyes sparkled. "Oh, you."

Sophie laughed and kissed Grandma on the cheek once again before joining David and Troy in the car. "Off we go," she said and put the SUV into reverse.

The drive to the church Grandma attended took ten minutes. Traffic was relatively light as they passed through the heart of the city, but she knew by the time they made the trek back it would be congested with the lunchtime rush and holiday shoppers coming to buy their gifts at the city's sprawling shopping center in the middle of town.

The streets and outer windows of the stores and restaurants were decorated with snowflake-shaped lights and green garlands. Though she'd already shopped online and had gifts sent to her parents and siblings, she needed to do some more Christmas shopping so that Grandma had other gifts beside the fuchsia-colored silk scarf she'd bought on Gran Canaria Island.

And something more for Troy and a gift for David as well. Though what she could possibly get for David was beyond her. A tie, maybe?

"Uncle David, that's where you used to live!" Troy exclaimed from the backseat.

David leaned forward and craned his neck to look upward through the front windshield. "Yep." He sat back and looked at her. "I had the corner unit on the sixteenth floor."

At the stoplight, Sophie dipped her head to stare up at the towering, modern apartment building. Winter sun gleamed off the windows. "You had a good view."

"We could see Lake Samish," Troy said.

David chuckled. "That's right. Lake Sammamish."

Sophie recognized the name and remembered summers going to the freshwater lake only eight miles away from Grandma's house. "Nice. Do you miss it?"

David seemed to consider her words. "Not really. I'm where I'm supposed to be."

It thrilled and pleased her to hear him say that. She admired and respected his commitment to his nephew. And to his company. She was really proud of him for giving his staff some paid time off when he could easily have not.

He twisted around to say to Troy, "What's your favorite Christmas song?"

"'Rudolph'!" came Troy's enthusiastic answer.

David and Troy sang Christmas songs, their voices filling the SUV. Sophie tapped a finger in rhythm on the steering wheel, marveling how different David was today. Relaxed and buoyant.

Sophie had a hard time reconciling this man with the one from yesterday who'd been tense and terse. But maybe sharing his past with her had lifted some of the stress from his shoulders?

She hoped so. For his and Troy's sake. They deserved to be happy. She wanted them to be happy. And though she was leaving soon, David and Troy would still live next to Grandma. It would be good for all of them to have each other.

"Hey," Sophie broke into the boys' rendition of "Jingle Bells" as Grandma's request popped into her mind.

David stopped singing and winced. "That bad, huh?"

"What?" Oh, he thought she didn't like his singing. "Quite the contrary. You have a very pleasant voice." She looked in the rearview mirror and smiled at Troy. "Both of you do. Must be a Murphy thing."

"A Murphy thing!" Troy cheered.

"I like that," David said.

"I aim to please," she quipped, and then blushed as he dipped his chin and arched an eyebrow. "How do you even know those songs?"

"Sitting around the fireplace with the family belting out silly Christmas songs didn't cost anything," he said quietly.

She met his steel gray gaze and had no response. The concept of her family gathered around the fireplace and singing together was such a foreign concept. His childhood was so much richer than hers in ways she'd never imagined. He had a depth to him she hadn't expected. She liked that he felt so comfortable and confident in sharing his voice with her and Troy.

"Grandma wanted me to ask you and Troy to dinner tonight. She's invited a friend." She dropped the volume of her voice to add, "A male friend."

"Really?" David shifted in the seat to face her. "Way to go, Grandma."

Sophie chuckled. "My thoughts exactly. Only Grams is a little nervous about the whole thing."

"So we'd be a nice buffer in case it's awkward," he said.

She gave him a startled glance. "I was thinking the same thing."

He grinned and wagged his eyebrows at her. "We're in sync."

She swallowed, though her tongue felt glued to the roof of her mouth and she had to force herself to look straight ahead.

We're in sync. The words bounced through her, shredding her up inside. She couldn't be in sync with him. That would be bad. Wouldn't it?

She pulled into the parking lot of the church and drove around to the back as Grandma had told her to do. She parked near the back door of the A-frame church building nestled among a lush evergreen landscape. "I'll go in and see where we're supposed to take everything."

David winked. "We'll be waiting."

Taken aback by his playful mood, she wasn't sure how to respond, so she didn't. She hurried inside and asked the church secretary for directions. Armed with instructions, Sophie returned to the car to find David and Troy already unloading packages onto a rolling cart.

Another man helped to take the gifts from the back of the SUV. He looked to be in his late twenties, with ginger-colored, short-cropped hair and freckles on his boyish face. He had on jeans and a Seahawks sweatshirt.

He noticed Sophie and stopped to hold out his hand. "You must be Sophie," he said. "I'm Jeff, the youth pastor. Simon Bichon called and said you'd be coming by today with presents for the Christmas gift drive."

Obviously, Grandma and Simon had been talking. Sophie envisioned the pair in late-night chats on the phone. The image made her smile. "Hello, Pastor Jeff. Nice to meet you." She shook his hand. "The secretary said to put the presents in the great room?"

"I'll show you the way." He led them inside to the back of the church.

David pushed the rolling cart. Troy skipped alongside, and Sophie had to double her steps to keep up. They entered a large carpeted space with folding tables propped against the back wall and chairs stacked high in the corner. A small stage sat at the far end, along with a set of drums and a piano. There were five large bins holding brightly wrapped gifts lined up in the center of the room. Each one was labeled with an age group.

"This is the youth sanctuary," Pastor Jeff told them. "On

Christmas Eve we'll hold a Christmas party here for the community's underprivileged children. Our youth will serve them cookies and punch and hand out presents. We'll also have a craft station and caroling with our youth band."

"It's really a nice thing you're doing here," Sophie told him.

"Thank you," Jeff said. "I can't take credit, though. A group of the older teens in the youth group came up with the idea. They wanted a way to give back and have fun at the same time."

Sophie glanced at David. He'd wheeled the cart close to the bins. He and Troy were sorting the presents into the appropriate age containers. His expression was unreadable as he worked, but she knew he'd heard the pastor. What did David think about it all?

"Did you keep your receipts?" the pastor asked. "You can write off your purchases as a charitable tax deduction."

"Oh. I hadn't thought of that. I'll have to round them up."

"When you have them, drop them at the front desk. Shirley will give you the proper paperwork."

"Great. Thank you."

"No, thank *you*." Pastor Jeff moved to help Troy. "The younger youth group is putting on a Christmas pageant during the evening service. Troy, would you like to be a shepherd? We're short one."

Troy's face lit up. He whipped around to David. "Can I, Uncle David? Pleasssse?"

David's smile was full of love. "Of course. You'd make an awesome shepherd."

Troy beamed. "Can Riggs come, too?"

"Who's Riggs?" Pastor Jeff asked.

Sophie shared an amused glance with David. "Riggs is my grandmother's puppy. He's a ten-month-old Bernese mountain dog."

"He has a set of antlers," Troy supplied. "He could be my reindeer."

"Is Riggs well behaved?" the pastor asked.

"He is, but he's also still a puppy," Sophie cautioned. He couldn't really be considering Troy's request, could he? "Big and a bit clumsy."

"I don't think reindeer attended Jesus' birth," David said and ruffled Troy's hair.

Pastor Jeff grinned. "Though you're probably right, we'd love to have Riggs join us. I'm sure the puppy would do fine with the goat that one of the other little girls is bringing. We'll have our own menagerie."

"Yes!" Troy danced in a circle.

Sophie stared at the pastor. "Are you sure?"

"He'll be on a leash, right?"

"Yes."

"Great."

"Is there a practice you'll need him to attend?"

The pastor laughed. "The show is pretty self-explanatory. We'll do a quick run-through just before, but that's all we'll really need."

"Great. So what time do we need to be here?" David asked with a smile.

"The Christmas party starts at four and the service starts at six. So as long as you arrive by five, we'll be good."

Troy grabbed David's hand. "Can we come for the party, too?"

Sophie bit her lip as she watched dismay march across David's face.

She was about to offer to bring Troy in his stead when David said, "We'll see. Let me think about it."

Troy scrunched up his face. "Pleasssse."

"Troy, I said I'd think about it." David's voice held an edge to it.

Troy stuck out a lip. He looked so adorably miffed that Sophie had to suppress a smile. Knowing what she did about David's past, she wanted to spare him from having to argue with Troy but wasn't sure how. Instead she asked, "What about a costume?"

Troy perked up. "I get to wear a costume?"

She turned to the pastor. "What should he wear?"

The pastor's gaze bounced between them, then settled on her. "An old sheet with a rope belt would suffice."

"I think we can manage that," she said, and glanced at David. He watched her with an interest that made her pulse pound. "We should be heading home now."

He slowly nodded.

"Again, thank you for your generosity," Pastor Jeff said as he shook their hands.

They left the pastor in the great room. Troy slipped his hand into Sophie's as they made their way down the hallway behind David. The gesture twisted her stomach into knots. His tiny little hand was warm and trusting within hers. Tender affection swelled within her heart. She had to fight to breathe through the tide of maternal yearning surging from someplace deep within.

Confused and panicked, she told herself she wasn't ready for this. For loving Troy and wishing he were hers. What had she been thinking to ever let herself get this close? But she couldn't bring herself to pull her hand away.

David held open the door for them to exit the church building. His eyebrows raised as his gaze moved from Troy and Sophie's joined hands to meet Sophie's gaze.

The intensity in his steel gray eyes made her mouth go dry. She didn't need to read his mind to understand the worry pinching his brows together. He was afraid Troy was becoming too attached to her.

And she worried she was becoming too attached to both Troy and David.

Time to shore up her defenses and remember this was only a pleasant interlude. This was not something that would last beyond the holidays. No matter how desolate the knowledge left her feeling.

CHAPTER 10

"Wow, little dude. Dressing to impress." David stopped in the doorway of Troy's room. They were getting ready to go next door for dinner with the ladies and Louise's male friend. Troy had taken a bath and then insisted on dressing himself. He wore a pair of chinos, a denim button-down shirt, and brown loafers.

Troy grinned. "I want to look nice for Sophie."

David nearly groaned at the innocent words that cut through him like a two-edged blade. His nephew was falling for Sophie big time. David didn't blame him. She was beautiful, fun, and sweet. He'd really enjoyed spending time with her today. And when he'd seen Troy and her holding hands, he'd had to fight the urge to take her other hand. He was getting in too deep. They both were. David needed to pull Troy, and himself, back from the edge of the cliff they were on the brink of careening over.

Troy canted his head. "Aren't you going to change?"

David glanced down at the jeans and hoodie he'd put on before they'd gone to the church. He'd planned to go as is, but now he reconsidered. Maybe he should put on something a little less casual.

He gave his nephew a lopsided smile. "I suppose I will." He moved into the room and sat on the bed. "But first I need to talk to you about something." He opened his arms and Troy moved to sit on his knee and wrap his arms around David's neck.

"You remember we talked about Sophie leaving after the holidays, right?" David asked.

"Yes. She's going to take pictures. That's what she does. She's a photographer."

Sophie must have talked to him about her trip as well. Okay. Good. Troy got that she wasn't staying. "Right. Her job takes her all over the world." David brushed back Troy's hair from his forehead. "I want to make sure you don't get hurt."

Troy drew back. "Hurt? I'm real careful. I look both ways before crossing the street. I don't use knives." The earnest expression on his little face made David's heart ache. "They are for grown-ups. I don't touch the stove either. It could be hot."

David pressed his lips together to keep his smile under control. He sought for a serious expression. "All good things to remember."

"That's what Sophie said."

David sighed. "She's a smart lady. But she's not going to be here much longer. I know you'll be sad when she's gone."

Troy nodded. "Won't you, too?"

Sucking in a sharp breath, David searched his heart for the answer. "Yes. Yes, I will. We're friends, and it's always hard when our friends go away."

A frown pinched Troy's eyebrows. "But she's not going away forever. Not like Mommy and Daddy. Sophie will come back, right?"

The burn of tears welled up in his eyes. Troy was so innocent and loving. "I'm sure she will come to visit."

Troy brightened. "She has to. Her grandma lives next door. And when Sophie is here, she can take care of me. I like when she takes care of me."

David's stomach dropped. How did he make Troy understand that he shouldn't let Sophie into his heart? He decided he'd have to deal with the fallout when it happened. For now, he pulled Troy to his chest. "You're a great kid, you know that?"

"You're a great uncle." Troy squeezed him tight and then squirmed to be released. "Go change so we can go next door. Wear something nice."

"Aye, aye, Captain."

❋   ❋   ❋

"That was a fabulous meal," Simon Bichon declared.

"I'm happy to hear you enjoyed it," Grandma said. "It was a joint effort."

Sophie and Grandma shared a pleased look. "But it was your recipe, Grams. I just followed your directions." She couldn't help darting a glance in David's direction. She told herself she wasn't seeking his approval. Yeah, right. His focus was on his plate, however.

They sat around Grandma's dining room table. Christmas music played softly in the background. Grandma had wanted to use her good china. Banded in gold, the bone china dinnerware was festive against the red linen tablecloth. Candlelight flickered from gold-plated votive candles lining the center of the table and created shadow patterns on the sand and russet floral damask wallpaper lining the dining room. The evening had progressed with surprising ease. Riggs had given his approval of Simon with a slobbery kiss before settling on his bed to watch over them.

Sophie also approved of Simon. He was a very personable and likable gentleman with silver hair and twinkling light blue eyes that softened every time he looked at Grandma. Sophie couldn't be happier for Grams.

A tug at her sleeve drew Sophie's attention to Troy, who'd insisted on sitting beside her. "Yes, sweetie?"

"Can I have some more enchilas?" he asked. "They're good."

"*Enchiladas*," Sophie corrected with a chuckle and met David's gaze across the table. This time he was looking at her. He nodded with a soft smile. He looked handsome in his blue-and-white-striped button-down shirt, open at the collar, and khaki pants. She dragged her gaze from him to dish out the last piece of sour cream enchilada onto Troy's plate.

"I notice you don't have a Christmas tree," Simon pointed out. "Do you need help procuring one?"

"David has offered to accompany us tomorrow to Sleigh Bells tree farm to pick out one," Grandma said. "He has a truck."

"Ah, I see." Simon glanced at David. "That's kind of you."

"It's the least I can do in return for all the ladies have done for Troy and me," David said.

Sophie bit back the unexpected stab of disappointment his words caused. He still insisted he owed them something for spending time with Troy. It saddened her to think David went through life always feeling the burden to repay every kindness sent his way. Why couldn't he just be grateful and accept generosity?

And why did she care?

For Troy's sake, she told herself. The boy was so sweet and bighearted. She'd hate to see him lose that by adopting his uncle's closed-off attitude.

"Would you mind if I impose and ask if I could join you on your Christmas tree hunt?" Simon asked, his gaze on Grandma.

She blushed under his intent regard. "Of course we'd love for you to come along."

Sophie was getting a kick out of Simon's obvious affection for Grandma. He was an interesting man. A venture capitalist, he'd told them earlier when David had asked. The two men had a lot in common, as they'd found out as they'd chatted stocks, bonds, and best practices for running a business.

"Who's ready for some dessert?" Sophie asked. "We made Grandma's award-winning persimmon cookies. They go great with a scoop of vanilla ice cream."

"Me," Troy promptly stated.

"That sounds delicious," Simon said.

Sophie stood and gathered her empty plate and the empty casserole dish.

David rose as well. "Troy, let's help Sophie clear the table."

Troy scrambled from his chair and grabbed his plate and utensils.

"Thank you," Sophie said to David when their gazes collided. Her pulse skipped a beat.

He smiled and stacked Grandma and Simon's empty plates on his and followed her out of the room.

In the kitchen, Sophie began dishing out ice cream onto small plates and added three warm, round persimmon cookies to each. David rinsed the dirty dishes and placed them in the dishwasher.

She handed a plate to Troy. "Can you give this to Grandma?"

The boy nodded solemnly and carefully carried the plate into the dining room.

"You're so good with him," David commented.

That was the second time he'd made the observation. Sophie was pleased he thought so. "He's really a great kid, you know."

"He's so much like my brother." David shut the dishwasher door and leaned against the counter. "Daniel loved to help people. He loved and lived with enthusiasm and without fear."

"You admired him," she said softly.

"I did. He was a much better person than I am."

She moved toward him and placed her hand on his forearm. "Don't sell yourself short. You're a good man, David. You have a lot of love to give and Troy needs that."

He covered her hand with his. "What do you need?"

She slipped her hand from beneath his but didn't move away. "Me?"

She gave a nervous laugh. Was he asking her if she needed love? How did she respond to that? "I'm good." She cringed at the squeak in her voice.

"Here." She shoved two plates with the dessert from the counter into his hands, then grabbed the other two plates and high-tailed it out of the kitchen with David's soft chuckle chasing her.

❄   ❄   ❄

David lifted a sleeping Troy from the couch in Louise's living room. It was time for them to go home and let the ladies get their beauty sleep. Not that either Louise or Sophie had a problem in that department. Okay, maybe he was a bit biased. He'd come to care for the Griffith women.

The evening had turned out very well. David approved of Simon. The man was intelligent and genuine and his devotion to Louise was unmistakable. And there was no denying the affection in Louise's gaze when she looked at Simon.

It stirred envy within David. He wanted that. He wanted to be devoted to a woman and have that devotion returned. But there wasn't room for a woman in his life. With his work and Troy, how could he make room for more? His gaze strayed from Troy in his arms to Sophie, who was tucking Troy's coat around the sleeping child.

David wanted Sophie. The thought rocked him back a step. But it would never work between them. They were two speeding trains headed in opposite directions.

Her eyebrows rose in concern. "Everything okay?"

He regained his balance. "Yes. We'll see you in the morning." He strode toward the front door. She hurried ahead of him to open the door.

He paused in the doorway. "Thank you for dinner. This was a really nice evening."

The hall light spilled over her hair. The strands looked soft and silky. He was glad he had his arms full or he might have reached out to slide his fingers through her pretty hair. And draw her closer to place a kiss on her lips.

"You're welcome, David." She went on tiptoe and leaned in.

His breath stalled. For a moment he thought she was going to kiss his cheek, but then she kissed Troy's forehead. A ribbon of jealousy wound through him and he mentally chastised himself for the ridiculous emotion. How could he be jealous of his nephew? Just because Troy received the affection David craved was no reason for the awful feeling making his stomach roil.

"Good night." Sophie stepped back. "We'll see you in the morning."

"In the morning," he repeated.

He couldn't wait for the sun to rise so he could see Sophie again. How crazy was that?

❄　　❄　　❄

Saturday morning dawned bright, with a winter sun that glistened on the dew left from the past few days of rain. A nice break but the sun in the Pacific Northwest was a fickle thing. Clouds could roll in without warning and rain was always expected.

Excitement fluttered through Sophie as she dressed in layers for the trip to the tree farm. She found Grandma in the kitchen, pouring coffee. She was getting around better on the crutches the past day or so.

Sophie never ceased to be amazed by her grandmother's strength and energy. Sophie couldn't say she was glad Grandma had pulled the ruse of needing help as a disguise for her matchmaking, but she could honestly say she was thankful for this time with her grandma. Today Grandma was dressed in a pair of slimming black waterproof pants and a pretty light blue sweater that matched the color of her eyes. Her silver hair had been brushed to a nice sheen. She looked younger than her age and Sophie hoped that she'd age as well.

"Don't you look nice," Grandma said, sliding a cup of coffee across the counter to Sophie. "That peach color is perfect for your complexion and makes your eyes even bluer."

"Between the base layer beneath my weatherproof walking pants, this sweater, and all the good food we've been eating"— Sophie put her arms out to her sides—"I feel like the little boy in *A Christmas Story* who can't put his arms down."

"Nonsense; you're beautiful." Grandma chuckled. "Well, maybe I can see it a little. Only you're taller than Ralph. We should watch that movie tonight. Troy will love it."

Would David think she was beautiful?

Oh, bother. Where did that thought come from? She needed to think about something other than David. "Are you happy that Simon is coming with us today?"

Grandma leaned on the crutches. Her smile was dreamy and made Sophie grin.

"Yes," Grandma admitted. "I really like him."

"And it's obvious he likes you." Sophie buttered the toast, set them on plates, and took them to the dining room table.

"But at our age?" Grandma hobbled to a chair and sat.

"Yes, at your age." Sophie took her hand. "You deserve to be happy, Grams. There is nothing wrong with you finding love."

Grandma patted her hand. "Maybe. We'll see."

Just as they finished their toast, the doorbell rang. Sophie wiped her mouth to make sure there were no crumbs and hurried to open the door. Simon stood there with two bouquets of flowers: red roses and Gerbera daisies. He was dressed for the outdoors with a rain hat, a shearling-lined jacket, and heavy-duty pants tucked into rain boots.

"Hello. Come in," Sophie said, moving back so he could enter.

"Good morning." He held out the bouquet of brightly colored Gerbera daisies to her. "For you."

She took the flowers. "They're beautiful. Thank you."

He nodded to Sophie, but he was already heading to Grandma with the bouquet of red roses.

Sophie ached with joy as she watched the delight lighting up Grandma's face. Simon bent and kissed her cheek in greeting.

"Are those for us?" a deep voice said behind Sophie. Startled, she whipped around to the still-open door and found David and Troy standing there looking so handsome and sweet that her heart sighed with its own special kind of joy. They both had on jeans and warm sweaters beneath their rain gear.

She laughed. "These are from Simon." Gathering herself, she gestured for them to come in. "We'll be ready to leave in a moment."

While they all greeted each other, she took the two bouquets of flowers and put them in vases, then set them on the dining room table.

"You're prettier than the flowers," David said as he joined her in the dining room.

A blush worked its way up her neck and settled in her cheeks. "Thank you."

Troy ran into the room. "Can we go now?"

David ruffled his hair. "Yep. Time to go."

Sophie grabbed Riggs's leash and attached it to his collar, grabbed her camera, and followed everyone outside.

They ended up taking two cars—Simon and Grandma in Simon's sedan, while Sophie and Riggs joined David and Troy in David's truck.

When they arrived at the farm, they met up at the front gate. Sleigh Bells Christmas tree farm was north of Bellevue on ninety acres. The sea of green trees was a beautiful contrast to the urban high-rise skyline in the distance. The air was heavy with the scent of pine. Hidden speakers played cheery Christmas music.

Simon pushed Grandma's wheelchair, since she'd elected to leave the crutches in the car. Riggs's attention was divided between smelling the ground, trees, and bushes and watching over her. He would trot to the end of the leash and then back to Grandma's side, which meant Sophie stayed close to Grandma.

Grams took the brochure the gate attendant handed her. "Where to first?"

"The animals." Troy pulled at David's hand. "There they are." He pointed toward a fenced pen beneath a tented roof. The petting zoo had goats, sheep, and a baby llama.

"Okay, buddy, hold on," David told him. "Let's see what every-one else would like to do."

They all looked up as they heard the jingle of the wagon drawn by two beautiful roans coming down the dirt lane through the rows of Christmas trees. Riggs barked at the strange sight. Sophie put her hand on his head to calm him. The horses didn't seem to care about the dog, and the wagon drew to a halt near the front gate.

"That looks like my speed," Grandma quipped. "A nice hay ride."

Simon put his hand on Grandma's shoulder. "Shall we?"

"Please." Grandma looked to Sophie. "You don't mind picking out the tree without us, do you?"

Sophie laughed, glad to see Grandma enjoying herself. "Not at all. We'll meet you back here for donuts and coffee a little later."

Simon wheeled Grandma toward the sleigh. Riggs followed, but Sophie reined him in. "You're staying with me, boy."

"I guess it's just the four of us," David said softly, drawing her focus to him.

The four of them. For now. She felt a pang because she'd be leaving soon. That was what she wanted, right?

Yes, it was. She wanted the job in the Alps and what it could mean for her career. But until she left she'd enjoy this time with David and Troy. She smiled brightly. "Looks like it."

"Can we please go see the animals now?" Impatience threaded through Troy's voice.

Sophie and David shared a laugh and hurried with Troy to the petting zoo. Sophie tightened her hold on the leash, expecting Riggs to raise a fuss at the other creatures, but he was content to sniff the ground, totally ignoring the cry of the goats and the bleating of the sheep.

She and David leaned against the railing of the pen as Troy

went inside to pet the animals. He was tentative at first but then he grew more comfortable. One of the farm's workers handed him a brush, and Troy used it on a cute black lamb that seemed to like the attention.

"How tall of a tree do you want?" David asked. He had the brochure out and was looking at the map of where the various types of trees the farm grew were located.

"Not quite ceiling height," she answered, picturing how a tree would look in Grandma's living room.

"That's what I was thinking, too. What type? They have a dozen different varieties."

"Hmmm. Normal type?" Her parents put up the same kind of tree every year in their entryway. The tree towered above them at nearly twelve feet tall. Though the tree always looked lovely, Sophie had never felt much excitement at the prospect of a Christmas tree.

Probably because her parents hired someone else to decorate it. It had never been a family event. But this year, Sophie and Grandma would decorate the tree together, and that was worthy of Sophie's excitement.

Glancing up, he said, "Well, do you like fuller limbs, or do you like the kind that looks like layers of limbs?"

"Fuller."

"Me, too. I prefer the Douglas fir. But the spruce is popular, too."

"I'm fine with Douglas." Not that she knew the difference.

"Great." He pointed to a section on the map near the back of the farm. "It says these Douglas fir trees are under seven feet but over five feet. That's where we should head."

"Sounds good." Sophie had to admit she was content just being here with David, watching the delight on Troy's face.

"All the trees are numbered, so once we decide on the trees we want, we give them the number and they will send someone out to cut it down." He was reading from the paper they'd given him when they came in. "They will wrap it up and load it on the truck," he said, sounding relieved.

"You're not going to cut it down yourself?" she teased.

He lifted his gaze. His eyes widened. "I could. They give you that option. Would you rather I do it?"

He looked so stricken by the idea she giggled. "No. I think having them do the dirty work, so to speak, is the way to go."

He grinned. "I was hoping you'd say that."

When Troy had his fill of the animals, they left the petting zoo and stopped at the small wooden structure that housed the bathroom so Troy could wash his hands before making the trek to the back of the farm. The smell of pine in the air thickened. Clouds rolled across the sky. Though the rain held off, the ground was muddy and slippery.

"Okay, these are the trees we should choose from," David said, stopping at a crop of trees with red tags.

David and Troy inspected each tree while Sophie and Riggs walked around several, looking at the shape and color of the different trees. Every so often, she'd glance over to find David watching her. He'd smile, then look away. It became a game of sorts. She'd step behind a tree for a moment, then step around it to find David looking in her direction. After several times, she came around a tree but David and Troy were gone.

She frowned and searched for them but couldn't see them anywhere. Had they left her and Riggs? A sinking feeling in the pit of her stomach made her shoulders bunch with tension. Her heart raced. She hadn't felt this sensation in a very long time.

Not since the days when her brothers would ditch her for

sport. She didn't like this feeling, or the fact that she'd allowed David to have this kind of power over her. She didn't let anyone get close enough to ditch her. Not like this. Not so that it hurt.

Realization pounded through her, trapping her breath in her lungs. She'd been dumped before—more than a couple times, in fact—but she'd never really been hurt. Not the deep, down, torn-up-heart kind of hurt. What did that say about her?

She felt a tap on her shoulder and spun around to find David and Troy behind her. How had they snuck up on her like that? She sent Riggs a sharp glance. The traitorous dog hadn't warned her they were there.

"Did you pick out a tree?" David asked.

She blinked. A tree? Oh, right. "Yes." She pointed to the closest one. "This one."

He took the tag off the tree's limb. "We found ours, too. Shall we head back for some hot cocoa and donuts while we wait for the trees to be brought to the truck?"

"Yippeee! Donuts!" Troy shouted.

Riggs barked, clearly wondering what was so exciting.

Sophie's pulse slowed, coming closer to normal. She was in so much trouble. She was well on her way to falling for David and she didn't know how to stop it. Did she want to stop it? But what would that mean? How would falling for David affect her future? Her career?

They were silly questions that had no answer. Because it didn't matter if she fell head over heels in love with the man. He wasn't a part of her plan. She needed to keep focused on the goal.

Which was? a tiny voice inside her head whispered.

To win her parents' and siblings' respect by becoming the most sought-after, prestigious photographer possible.

Why did that leave her feeling so cold inside? It never had before.

It had to be the weather chilling her bones.

"You okay?" David peered at her with concern.

She forced a smile. "Yes. Fine. Donuts, here we come."

❄ ❄ ❄

David grabbed a napkin to wipe powdered sugar off Troy's face. They sat with Sophie, Simon, and Louise in the warming hut, holding cups of hot chocolate and a few dozen freshly made donuts. Ever since they'd returned from picking out their trees, Sophie had been strangely quiet. Had he done something again to offend her?

"What are your plans for this evening?" Simon asked.

David glanced at the other man and realized his question was for all of them.

"No plans," Louise said. She turned to Sophie. "Do we?"

Sophie seemed to be lost in thought, staring into her cocoa.

"Soph?" Louise touched her hand. "Earth to Sophie."

Sophie lifted her gaze. "Hmm? Oh, tonight. No plans."

"David, are you and Troy available?" Simon asked.

"Sure. What do you have in mind?"

"I'd like you all to join me for dinner at Ferralla's restaurant," Simon said. "We could watch the Snowflake parade."

"Yes, the parade. Can we?" Troy piped up.

Pleased by the invitation, David nodded. "We'd like that."

"Ladies?" Simon's hopeful expression was all for Louise.

Louise touched his hand. "That's so thoughtful of you to offer. I'd love to. Sophie?"

"Yes," she said distractedly. "That'd be great." She tilted her head. "Wait. A parade?"

"The Snowflake parade runs through downtown Bellevue nightly through the Christmas season," Simon explained.

Sophie turned to David. "Did you know this?"

He chuckled. "I used to live on the route, remember? Troy and I hit the parade the first night it opened but we'd love to see it again. Right, buddy?"

"Yep. I want to see Olaf again," Troy said. "He's funny."

"Olaf is an animated character from a children's movie," David told Sophie.

She arched an eyebrow but there was a twinkle in her blue eyes. "I know who Olaf is, silly. He's a bear, right?"

"Nooo," Troy said. "He's a snowman."

"A snowman?" Sophie peered at Troy. "Are you sure Olaf isn't a dinosaur?"

Troy exploded with laughter. "You're thinking of Barney."

"Ah." Sophie laughed. "I can't wait to see Olaf then."

"Have you never seen *Frozen*?" Troy asked, his little face so stunned that David had to chuckle.

"Hmmm." Sophie put her index finger on her chin. "Can't say that I have."

"Uncle David, we have to show Sophie *Frozen*."

"A definite must," David agreed and held her gaze. "For another night."

"Another night," she whispered.

And he took that as a promise.

"David?" a familiar female voice spoke from behind him.

Tensing, David swiveled in his chair to find a tall, pretty redhead smiling at him. "Libby. Hello. What are you doing here?"

Her curious green-eyed gaze swept over the group, pausing slightly on Sophie and Troy before swinging back to him. "Getting a Christmas tree." She gave a laugh, but it sounded forced. "Is this your family?"

He cringed at the slight hint of hurt in her tone. They'd dated a few years earlier, right after he'd started his company. She'd wanted more out of the relationship than he was willing to give, so it had ended pretty soon after it started.

He put his hand on Troy's shoulder. "This is my nephew, and these are our neighbors." David made the introductions. "This is Libby Hall."

Libby placed her manicured hand on his shoulder. The pale pink tips of her nails were a sharp contrast to his dark coat. "We're old friends." She smiled at him and leaned closer. "I've missed you."

David's jaw tightened with embarrassment. He had no response to her proclamation.

"Did you find a Christmas tree?" Sophie asked politely.

Libby darted a look in Sophie's direction. "Yes." She sized up Sophie and then immediately turned her gaze back to David.

"We should get together. Catch up," she said. Her hand lingered on his shoulder.

"Maybe we should sometime." He moved so her hand wasn't on him. "It's good to see you, Libby." David hoped she'd get the hint and leave.

She squeezed his shoulder. "You, too. I have the same number. Give me a call. I'd love to see you again."

He didn't have her number any longer and had no intention of calling. "Are you here alone?" That didn't seem like her at all.

She laughed, a throaty sound that grated on David's nerves. "No. I should get back to my date." She turned her gaze to the others. "It was nice meeting you."

"Likewise," Simon said.

Libby's hand touched his shoulder again. "David."

" 'Bye, Libby."

She walked away and David turned back to the table. He met Sophie's cool gaze.

"She seems nice," Sophie said.

"She is, I suppose. We dated for a short time. Nothing serious." At least for him it hadn't been.

"How about a visit to Santa?" Louise asked the group.

"Santa!" Troy clapped his hands. "Can we, Uncle David?"

Dragging his gaze away from Sophie, David smiled. "Of course. We can't go Christmas tree shopping without a stop by the man in the red suit's house."

"It's not his *real* house, Uncle David," Troy chided. "The real Santa lives at the North Pole."

"Good to know." David rose and held out his hand to Sophie. "Will you come with us?"

She hesitated a moment before slipping her hand into his and allowed him to draw her to her feet. "I don't want to miss Santa either."

He held onto her hand a moment, wondering if meeting Libby had given Sophie the wrong idea. He had no intentions of pursuing anything with Libby, but now was not the time to address that with Sophie.

After clearing away their cups and napkins, David tousled Troy's hair. "Let's wash your hands so you don't get cinnamon sugar in Santa's beard."

Troy stared at his hands, then dusted them off on his jeans. "They're clean."

"Now they are." Sophie's chuckle warmed David's heart. He met her gaze with a shrug. "Good enough?"

She nodded. "I'm sure Santa's used to sticky hands."

"All righty, then. Off to Santa's." David consulted the Christmas tree farm's brochure. "Santa's house is near the front gate, which will work out perfectly." A nice way to end the day.

Simon pushed Louise's wheelchair and David captured Troy's hand and held Riggs's leash in the other as they made their way from the warm concessions tent. Sophie jogged ahead a few feet and turned to take pictures.

"How about I take a few of you with your grandma and Simon," David offered.

"That would be great," Sophie replied.

"Here, Troy, take my hand." Louise held out her hand to Troy. Simon took Riggs's leash.

David transferred Troy to Louise's care and strode forward. Sophie removed the camera strap from around her neck. "It's all set up. All you have to do is point and shoot."

"Nice." He took the camera from her hands. He was surprised by its weight. He slipped the camera's strap over his neck so as not to risk dropping the thing. He couldn't imagine the price tag on such a nice piece of equipment. He had only his phone for taking pictures.

Sophie stepped beside her grandma, with Troy standing in front of her. She put her hand on his shoulder like a mother would with her son. David's stomach clenched at the sight.

"Maybe I should step out," Simon offered.

Louise reached up to take his arm. "Please don't."

The older man smiled down at Louise with tender affection while Riggs put his head onto Louise's lap. David snapped off a shot. It was a heady feeling, knowing he'd immortalized the moment.

"Smile for the camera." David raised his voice to get their attention.

He took several shots, hoping they would turn out okay.

"Here, young man, let me take one with you and your family," said an older man wearing a jacket with the tree farm's logo on it as he approached David.

David blinked back his surprise. The thought of correcting the man's assumption skimmed at the edge of his mind. But it wasn't necessary to explain they weren't family, only neighbors. Yet the idea of them being one big family made his heart ache with a strange yearning that he chose to ignore. Instead, he looked to Sophie for an answer. She gave him a nod of consent.

After handing over the camera and ensuring the man had the strap securely around his neck, David jogged back to the group and took his place next to Sophie. He put his hand to the small of her back. She glanced at him with a startled smile but didn't shift away.

"One, two, three," the man said. "Smile."

When the man rejoined them, he handed David the camera and then turned to Louise. "Louise Griffith, it's so nice to see you."

"Tucker," Louise said with a warm smile. "I wasn't sure you'd remember me. Tucker's family has owned the tree farm for several generations."

"How could I forget one of the prettiest girls in our high school graduating class?" Tucker's gaze shifted to Simon and back. "Ellie will be sad she missed seeing you today."

"Tell her hello for me," Louise said. "I really should call her. It would be such fun to reconnect. Where are my manners? Let me introduce you to my friend Simon Bichon." She obviously caught the curious look Tucker had sent Simon.

The two men shook hands. David couldn't help notice the way they sized each other up.

"And this is my granddaughter Sophie and our neighbors David and Troy Murphy. The overgrown pup is my dog Riggs."

Sophie, then David, shook Tucker's hand. Tucker smiled at Troy and petted Riggs.

"This is a nice place you have here," David said.

"Yes, it is," Sophie agreed. "Such a fun family environment."

"Thank you." Tucker appeared pleased by the compliment. "Did you all find Christmas trees?"

"We did. They are being cut and prepared to take home as we speak," David told him. "We're headed to Santa's house now."

The older man's eyes twinkled. "I won't keep you then."

He gave Riggs one last ruffle behind the ears and strode away toward the concessions tent, greeting people as he went.

David led the way past the busy entrance gate. A pole with a red-and-white sign pointed the way down a tree-lined path to a twelve-by-twelve red house nestled among the greenery. A ramp led up to a red door the color of Santa's suit, and wavy white molding reminiscent of Santa's beard welcomed them.

There was a line made up of children, mostly six and under, bundled against the cold in hats and mittens. The youngest ones were held by their parents. The line started at the front door and stretched down the path. They joined the line.

Overhead the early morning sun that had brightened the day had disappeared behind a mass of dark clouds rolling in from the west. The temperature dropped by several degrees. By the time they made it to the front of the line, a drizzle had started. David was glad the drier weather had held out as long as it had.

A woman dressed as an elf in red-and-white-striped fleece pants and a green jacket trimmed in white fur greeted them at the entrance. She wore green mud boots instead of curled-toed shoes. David paid the fee for Troy to go inside to have a picture taken with Santa.

"Can we come in, too?" Louise asked. She held up Riggs's leash.

"Of course." With a grand bow, the elf gestured for them all to crowd through the doorway.

Inside the small wood-paneled house a warm fire burned in a gas fireplace. A large reindeer antler chandelier hung overhead. A festively decorated Christmas tree surrounded by cheerily wrapped presents stood in the corner. In the center of the room sat Santa in all his red glory on a large, ornately carved wooden chair. The man's girth was what one expected of a Santa, and his white beard and bushy eyebrows appeared real to David.

"Ho, ho, ho," the man in red intoned. "Who do we have here?" He held out his hand to Troy.

Troy tightened his hand around David's and didn't move. His eyes were big and his mouth hung open.

David gently nudged Troy. "It's okay. Go on."

With an audible gulp, Troy slowly made his way to Santa's side. "Hi, Santa."

"What's your name?" Santa asked.

"Troy. Troy Murphy."

Santa patted his knee. "Climb on up here, child, and tell Santa what you wish to find under the Christmas tree."

As Troy settled on Santa's knee, Riggs strained against the leash, clearly wanting to be with Troy.

"Here's my elf assistant to take our picture," Santa said, gesturing to another elf, dressed exactly like the one at the door. Only this one stood behind a tripod set up with a Polaroid camera.

"Can Riggs have his picture taken, too?" Troy asked.

Hearing his name, Riggs let out a bark.

Santa laughed, a deep belly laugh that made them all smile. "Of course."

David situated Riggs next to Santa. The dog sat with his gaze on Troy. "Stay," David said but wasn't sure he even needed to give the command.

As the elf took a picture, Sophie snapped off several shots of her own.

"So cute," Louise said softly.

"Troy," Santa said after the elf was done, "what do you want for Christmas?"

Troy leaned in and whispered something into Santa's ear. Santa nodded, his brown eyes widening as he darted a glance toward the adults. David's stomach clenched. What had Troy asked for?

"Well, I'll see what I can do, but that might be more than even Santa can accomplish," the jolly man said.

Troy sighed and nodded. "I'm praying about it, too."

David's mouth went dry. What if Troy asked for his mom and dad back?

Santa smiled. "Good idea."

David let out a breath. The old man wouldn't have smiled if Troy had asked for something like that, would he? He met Sophie's gaze. He could tell she was thinking the same thing.

"Anything else?" Santa asked.

Troy considered then said, "Sodor Fire Station."

Relief loosed the constriction in David's chest. He could do Sodor Fire Station.

"What's that?" Sophie whispered.

"Another piece to the Thomas the Train track set." He grinned, remembering the night she'd gotten tangled up in the tracks.

"Ah." She nodded with a smile. She held his gaze, and he momentarily forgot where he was. David could lose himself in her eyes.

Troy hopped down from Santa's lap and launched himself at David. Scooping the boy into his arms, David said, "Tell Santa thank you."

"Thank you, Santa," Troy said.

"Come, Riggs," Louise called to the dog, who had his paws up on Santa's knee.

Santa scrubbed Riggs behind the ear. "Good boy."

Riggs hopped down and padded to Louise's side. Simon reattached the leash to Riggs's collar.

"This way, please," the elf said, ushering them out of the little house in the woods so another family could come inside.

Once they were outside and headed back to the main gate, where they'd pick up their trees, David asked Troy, "What did you tell Santa?"

Troy shook his head. "I can't tell you. It's a secret."

David wanted to press. He wanted to make sure that whatever Troy had asked for, he could provide. He hated the thought of Troy's hopes being dashed. But maybe there were some things David couldn't protect Troy from.

Or himself. David's gaze strayed to Sophie; she had her camera up and took his and Troy's picture. He had no idea how to protect himself from the feelings taking root in his heart for the beautiful photographer.

He was in big trouble.

CHAPTER 11

"We can see everything from here." Troy pressed his nose to the restaurant's large plate-glass window. He looked so cute in his sweater and khaki pants.

Ferralla's, famous for its Italian cuisine, sat right on the main drag that ran through the heart of Bellevue. Sophie had never eaten here before and was impressed by the ambience. Classical versions of well-loved Christmas tunes played over the speakers. Candles graced every linen-covered table, and the overhead lights glowed a soft, warm yellow.

They were seated at a window table on the second floor and had a perfect view of the street below. The snowflake-shaped lights strung along the trees lining the sidewalks twinkled in the evening air. People stood on both sides of the street in preparation for the Snowflake parade. The mall, a brick building with decorated arched windows, sat directly across the way, and it was busy with holiday shoppers.

She snapped off a few shots of Troy with his back to her. She swung the camera to David and took several pictures. He stuck his tongue out at her in most of them.

She rolled her eyes. "Stop, you goof."

He sat next to her looking handsome in dark slacks and a white shirt and red tie beneath a gray houndstooth sport jacket. His dark brown hair was spiked, like he'd run his fingers through it rather than using a comb. His strong jaw was shaven and the scent of his aftershave had been teasing her since he and Troy had stopped at the house to pick her up for their dinner with Grandma and Simon.

They'd again traveled in two cars, which meant Grandma and Simon had plenty of alone time. But so did she and David. Granted, Troy had been in his car seat, but he was reading a picture book adaptation of the movie *Frozen* and was completely uninterested in them.

On the ride over, she'd wanted so badly to ask about Libby. Did David intend to take up with her again?

The woman had clearly been interested in rekindling her relationship with him. The thought of them together crimped Sophie's heart.

But what did it matter to her if David called the redhead?

Sophie had no claim on David. Not now, not ever. So she'd stuffed her curiosity and the burn of jealousy down a dark hole.

"This is such a treat," Louise said, twirling her string of pearls. She'd worn a light blue dress and had her hair pulled up in a pearl-studded clip. She sat beside Simon, their plush chairs scooted close together.

Sophie took their picture, loving the way the camera captured their closeness, their ease with each other.

Waiters wearing black and white brought appetizers to the table and refilled their water glasses. Sophie tucked her camera back in its case so she could sample the food on the trays.

David shifted in his seat, his knee bumping hers, sending little tingles up her spine. She should move away, but the pleasant sensations were too good to let go of. "How did you get these seats on such short notice?" he asked Simon.

"I own half of the restaurant," Simon confessed with a half smile. "One of my investments."

As the two men discussed business stuff, Sophie relaxed, content to listen. She was impressed with Simon, not because he owned half the restaurant, but because he didn't flaunt his wealth. He came across as so down to earth. He was nothing like the affluent people who ran in her parents' circles. And she was also impressed with David for his prowess in keeping up in the conversation. Most of what they talked about—stocks and rates and such—went over her head.

She could break down a camera and put it back together. She could arrange lights and frames and create beautiful works of art. She could talk aperture, shutter speed, and IOS. But business? It was like listening to a language she didn't speak. That was why she had an agent, to deal with all that stuff.

Their dinner arrived, and it was as scrumptious as advertised. Sophie had ordered a melt-in-your-mouth lasagna. The rich meat and tomato sauce were delicious. She glanced up to see David's pleasure as he bit into his chicken Parmesan.

Their gazes locked. The corners of his mouth curved in a smile that made her pulse skip along her limbs. For a moment, it seemed that all else faded except the two of them. He picked up a slice of garlic bread from a wicker basket on the table and offered it to her. She took it, their fingers brushing together.

For some reason, that innocent touch sent off a maelstrom of sensation spiraling through her. Unaccountably, she wanted more. She wanted his fingers to slide along her arm, to tangle in her hair. She wanted to feel his lips on hers. She wanted the kiss she'd denied him.

"When does the parade start?" Troy asked with a mouthful of buttered noodles.

The moment shattered. Sophie dropped the bread onto her plate and sat back, her cheeks heating. Panicked by the yearnings coursing through her veins, she picked up her tea and forced her hands not to shake.

"No talking with food in your mouth," David admonished in a low tone.

Troy grimaced and swallowed, then opened his mouth to prove there was no more food inside. "Now can I ask?"

Sophie hid a smile behind her mug of hot tea.

David chuckled. "Yes, you may."

"How much longer until the parade starts? Can we watch it from down there?" Troy asked, pointing over his shoulder with his fork.

"We'll see," David responded. "Let's finish our meal first."

By the time dessert was served, a rich and creamy tiramisu, Sophie was stuffed.

Music rose from the street, signaling the beginning of the parade. Troy stood at the window. Sophie joined him. She needed to move after so much rich food. A marching band from the local high school kicked off the procession. Six kids wide and twenty deep, the band looked sharp in black pants, black coats, and yellow and white bibs. Tall, plumed hats sat perched on each teen's head. There were horns of every type and two rows of drums of various sizes. Sophie could feel the vibration of the music beating through her.

Troy took her hand. "Can we go down there?"

Her heart flipped in her chest. It felt so natural to have his small hand in her own. "We'll have to ask your uncle."

"I say let's go down there," David said as he stepped up behind them.

His breath stirred her hair. Awareness prickled her skin. He was so close, she could lean back into him with just the slightest shift in her stance. She held herself rigid, not wanting to give in to the warming of his presence, yet yearning to feel his arms around her again. She placed her free hand against the cool glass to ground herself. "I'd like that, too."

"I'll get our coats." David moved away to retrieve their outerwear from the coatroom.

Sophie tracked him with her gaze. He moved with such easy grace, with confidence and power. He was a man who commanded his world, who'd started a company and made it a success on his own. A man who'd taken in his orphaned nephew to raise. A man for her to admire, respect, and . . . she shied away from finishing that thought. She had a goal to focus on, and that goal didn't include a man and a child.

"We'll stay here where it's nice and cozy," Grandma said, drawing Sophie's focus.

Simon's arm rested across the back of Grandma's chair, where they sat with a good view of the happenings on the street below. They looked good together. Happy. Sophie was glad for that. "It is nice here. Thank you, Simon, for dinner. This was lovely."

"You're welcome, my dear," he replied with a pleased gleam in his blue eyes. "I'll make sure your grandmother gets home at a decent hour." He winked.

Grandma giggled. Sophie grinned.

David returned with their coats. He helped Sophie into hers, his hand lingering on her shoulders and making her tummy flutter. He bent down to help Troy with his jacket. They said their good-byes and headed down the interior staircase that took them to the main floor of the restaurant and out to the street. They wedged their way into a good spot where they could see the festivities.

A line of drummers from the junior high school dressed in blue and white warm-up suits ra-ta-ta-taed their way down the street, followed by a float decorated with red carnations and jingle bell dancers in sparkly red costumes and doing high kicks. Next came an old-fashioned fire engine loaded with firemen of all ages who jumped off to hand out treats to the children.

The temperature had dropped considerably. Sophie shivered as a chill snaked beneath the collar of her wool coat.

David slid an arm around her shoulders. "Cold?"

She couldn't help snuggling closer. For warmth, not because she'd been longing to get close to him. "A little."

Troy seemed impervious to the cold as he watched. He was no doubt waiting for his favorite character, Olaf, to appear. Girls twirled their batons in the air and spun around, their silvery costumes shimmering in the light from the snowflake decorations along the street.

Troy jumped up and down with glee. "There he is!"

Sure enough, a life-size version of the animated snowman character waddled down the street, waving and throwing candy to those gathered on the sidewalks.

Troy bolted, running out into the street.

Sophie lunged to grab him but missed. David lurched away from Sophie to follow Troy. He reached the boy just as Troy flung his arms around Olaf. The costumed character hugged him back, handed him some candy, and then gently steered him toward David.

Grinning from ear to ear, Troy skipped back to Sophie's side. "Look what he gave me."

"Troy, don't do that again." David's voice held a definite tremble. "You scared me."

Unabashed, Troy peered up at his uncle. "Sorry. But I wanted to give him a hug. For my mommy. He was her favorite."

Placing a hand over her heart, Sophie fought back a wave of tears. David, too, appeared choked up by the boy's words. "Why don't we go inside the mall to warm up a bit before heading home?" she managed to say around the lump in her throat.

David sent her a grateful smile. "I like that plan."

Troy happily gobbled up the candy, stuffing the wrappers into his pockets. By the time they reached the middle of the first department store his hands were a gummy mess.

"Uh, David," Sophie said, eyeing Troy's hands. "Maybe you should take him into the restroom and wash up."

"Right." David put a hand on Troy's thin shoulder. "Let's go, little man. Time to clean all the stickiness off."

"I'll wait here," Sophie offered. The display cases full of shiny jewelry caught her attention. Maybe she could pick up a little something for Grandma.

The boys walked away, leaving Sophie to browse. She found a pretty gold filigree scarf clip with a centerpiece of porcelain painted with a flower corsage. It would look lovely on the silk scarf she'd brought from Gran Canaria. She paid for it and was about to turn away when a silver charm bracelet drew her back to the case. "Can I see that?" she asked the salesclerk.

The clerk helped to secure it on her wrist.

Snowflake-shaped charms dangled and sparkled as she held out her arm to admire it. "How much is it?"

When the clerk told her, she quickly undid the clasp and

handed it back. She liked the piece and it would have reminded her of Troy and David and the Snowflake parade, but she wasn't into spending that much money on herself.

"That's beautiful." David's deep voice startled her.

She jerked around with a small laugh. "It is." She held up her bag. "I got Grams a gift. Now where to?"

They made their way into the body of the mall. Christmas carolers dressed in Victorian garb stood on a stage in the center of the promenade. They stopped to listen. Sophie let the words and the feeling of contentment seep into her bones.

With a start she realized she'd leaned back against David, and his arms held her loosely in his embrace. She told herself this was dangerous. He was dangerous. But she didn't want to move. She let the feel, the sensations imprint on her heart and her mind so that she'd have them when she left.

The carolers finished and everyone clapped, forcing David to remove his arms. Just as well, Sophie thought. Too much imprinting could lead to unwanted attachments.

Who was she kidding? She was attached to both Troy and David. But being attached didn't mean she was in love. Right?

❄   ❄   ❄

The next morning, David was up and ready for church before Troy. Considering Troy had once again slept through the night and David hadn't, David should have been fatigued, but his mind had been wound up with thoughts of Sophie. Yesterday had been perfect. They'd had fun together at the Christmas tree farm and later at dinner and then the parade. It had been just like a real family.

He should be scared by that thought. He knew she was leaving and he could tell himself to keep his heart under lock and key all he wanted, but it wouldn't change the fact that he'd grown to care deeply for Sophie.

And it wasn't just her physical beauty that drew him in, though there was that. She'd looked lovely last night in a dark green dress that hugged her curves, knee-high black boots, and a colorful headband holding back her hair, showing off her pretty face. But there was so much more to her. She was kind and generous. Smart and witty, too. He liked her confidence and her humility.

After church, David and Troy put up their Christmas tree, but David realized he didn't have many ornaments. There was a box of Troy's family's decorations in the storage facility where he'd placed all of Daniel and Beth's things when he'd cleaned out their condo. He hadn't been able to bring anything of theirs into the new house. There were too many memories and reminders of what both he and Troy had lost. Sorrow pinched his heart.

He wasn't sure if retrieving the familiar decorations was a good idea. He'd ask Sophie and see what she thought. She was so good at that sort of thing. She'd know if it would be harmful or helpful for Troy.

It occurred to him that he put a lot of stock in Sophie's opinions, especially in regard to Troy. But she was such a natural nurturer. She had a knack for parenting that David wished would rub off on him.

"Hey, buddy," David said to Troy, trying not to let his sorrow seep through his words, "let's go next door and see if the ladies need some help with their tree."

"Aren't we going to decorate our tree?" Troy asked. There was worry in his eyes.

"We will," David promised. He hated seeing the anxiety on

Troy's face. "But ladies come first." He scooped Troy into his arms.

"Okay, if you say so."

"I say so." David tickled Troy and the boy's laughter chased away the gloomy mood.

They headed to the Griffiths' house. Riggs barked as the two of them approached the front door, which opened before he could knock. Troy ran inside and tackled Riggs. The two tumbled on the floor and rolled around like two puppies.

Sophie greeted him with a smile. She'd changed from the pantsuit she'd worn to church. She looked comfortable in light-colored, well-worn jeans and a deep purple, long-sleeved athletic shirt. "I was just thinking about you two."

"You were?" David couldn't believe how much her words pleased him.

"Yes. Come in." She stepped out of the way. "It was good to see you at church this morning but I didn't get a chance to talk to you."

"You ladies were the center of attention." In fact, there'd been a big crush of people wanting to see Louise and meet her grand-daughter.

David had steered clear of the throng, deciding to vacate before he was drawn into the middle of people wanting to know who he was and his story. He preferred sitting in the back, where he could step out before anyone took it upon himself or herself to befriend him.

He'd slipped out to pick Troy up from his Sunday school class. The whole way home from church Troy had been full of chatter about the upcoming pageant.

Sophie wrinkled her nose. "That was a bit embarrassing."

"Nonsense," Louise huffed as she hobbled in on her crutches.

"Everyone loved you and was excited to meet you. I talk about Sophie a lot."

"Apparently," Sophie muttered with a smile. "Anyway, would you be willing to help me drag our Christmas tree from the garage to the living room? It's no longer dripping wet."

"That's why we're here." David headed for the garage. Behind him, he heard Troy say, "Our tree is up but not decorated. Ladies first."

David grinned with pride for his nephew. After fluffing the branches and making sure as many of the dead needles were off as he could, he carried the tree into the living room. Sophie had set up a stand in front of the window that looked out onto the street. Troy and Louise had disappeared into the kitchen. No doubt for a snack. David was happy to see that Troy's appetite was improving. As was his sleep. Troy hadn't had a nightmare last night.

"Can you steady it while I get the stem into the stand?" David asked Sophie.

She dove in to grab the trunk while David lay down and shuffled under the bottom branches to secure the end into the stand. When he wiggled his way out, Sophie giggled.

"What?"

"You have needles sticking out of your hair." Her eyes danced. "You look like a Chia pet."

He snorted. "I better shake them loose outside."

She followed him to the front yard. He bent over and shook his hair. A torrent of green fir needles fell around his feet. "Wow, you weren't kidding."

"Here." She stepped close and went on tiptoe to pluck a few stray pieces of greenery from his hair.

She was so close he could see the pulse point at her collarbone. He could smell the hint of vanilla in her shampoo. As she lowered from her tiptoes, their gazes met. Her breath hitched. His breathing turned shallow.

Yearning and longing converged, driving him to lower his head. He paused a scant measure from her lips. He braced himself in case she rejected his offer of a kiss again.

Only she didn't.

She pressed her mouth to his. Soft and pliant lips molded to his. He groaned and pulled her closer. Her hands gripped his shoulders. His hands delved into her silky hair, cradling her head as the kiss continued. An exploration, a giving and a taking. Soul-searing, heart-melting.

His senses sparked and popped. He'd had no idea a kiss could be so combustible. He was about to burn from the inside out and he didn't care. He craved the heat.

They broke apart, both struggling to catch their breath. He dropped his forehead to hers. "Wow."

She laughed, the sound so sweet it made his chest ache. "Wow is right. That was . . . electrifying."

He grinned. "My thought exactly."

"What are we doing?" she asked as her expression sobered.

"Does it matter?" he countered. "Can't we enjoy the time we have together? I know you're leaving. I would never ask you to stay. This isn't what you want in life. I get it. But Troy comes alive when you're around. I come alive when you're around. And as much as I want to protect Troy and myself from the heartache of you leaving, I think we're way past that point. That point was about five days ago."

She placed a hand over his heart. "You're asking a lot, you know? I may be the one brokenhearted when I go."

He captured her hand. "No, you won't. Neither of us is making promises or plans. And if kissing is too much, we don't have to do that again." His mouth quirked. "Though I won't deny I enjoy kissing you."

Her cheeks turned pink. "I like kissing you, too. But . . ."

He froze. "But?" Had he misread her feelings for him?

"I don't want to stand in the way if you want to renew your relationship with Libby."

"Libby?" He shook his head, wishing they'd never run into her. "I'm not interested in renewing anything with her. That's ancient history as far as I'm concerned."

Doubts swam in her blue eyes. "You're sure?"

"Positive." He slid an arm around her shoulders. "It's going to be okay. We have four more days until Christmas and then another week after that before you leave. Let's make the most of them."

Sophie's top teeth tugged at her bottom lip, drawing his attention. She nodded. "Okay."

He grinned. "Good. How about next week we take Troy and head up to Snoqualmie for some sledding and fun in the snow? It will give you a taste of what you'll be in for in the Alps."

"And the perfect excuse to buy a snow outfit."

"Exactly. We can go shopping for snow gear for all of us." He usually wasn't one to enjoy shopping, but with Sophie at his side he knew he would.

They went inside to decorate the Christmas tree. And David staunchly ignored the small voice in his head warning him that he was swimming in the deep end without a life jacket. He didn't want to be reminded of how easily he could drown.

CHAPTER 12

Sophie stepped back to admire the decorated Christmas tree and bumped into David. He steadied her, his hands on her shoulders. Though she'd regained her footing, he didn't drop his hands. She liked the way his touch through her sweater made her feel all tingly. The tree almost completely blocked Grandma's living room window, but it was so pretty, Sophie clapped in delight. "I love it."

"It is beautiful." Grandma leaned on her crutches and fingered an ornament, a gold and silver Nativity scene. "Your father gave this to me when he was a teen. He loved to buy me a new decoration every year. Still does." She touched another decoration, a porcelain snowflake with glitter in the glaze. "This is the one he sent last year."

Sophie hadn't known her father did that. It was such a sweet gesture.

David squeezed Sophie's shoulders and leaned in to whisper in her ear, "Can we talk privately?"

Her mouth went dry as she remembered what had happened the last time they talked in private. They'd kissed. And it had been wonderful and scary at the same time.

She still couldn't believe she'd agreed to let their relationship evolve into something beyond two ships set on different courses. She knew doing so would only prolong the agony when it was time to leave.

There was nowhere for a relationship between them to go. She was leaving. His life was here. Her life was a constant whirlwind of travel and jobs, while David's was grounded in raising his nephew and running a company.

Her only excuse for giving in to his request was that exhilarating and terrifying kiss they'd shared. It had opened the door to all the complicated feelings for David she'd been trying to keep at bay. She'd heard poets and novelists talk of romantic connections but never understood them.

Oh, she'd felt attraction, but this was something new. Something different. Deeper, more real. Maybe that was why her romantic relationships in the past had failed.

Her stomach dropped. Great. Just what she needed, to feel this deep-seated connection with the one man she shouldn't. She sent up a silent prayer to God for strength to resist falling in love with David.

But what if it is God's plan? a tiny voice inside her heart whispered.

She didn't want to contemplate all the implications of that thought, so she stepped away from David and gestured for him to follow her into the kitchen so they could talk.

Troy and Riggs sat on the floor side by side in front of the fire-place. Troy ate from a bowl of blueberries and the dog chewed on a bone. Grandma hobbled to the couch and plopped down with a sigh.

Sophie went to the kitchen sink to wash her hands. David followed her and placed a hand on either side of her, trapping her with his arms. She turned off the water and slowly spun to face him. She stared into his eyes. Something was bothering him. "What is it?"

In a low voice, he said, "I don't have Christmas ornaments. Daniel and Beth did. There are a couple of boxes full of decorations in the storage unit where I put all of their belongings. I'm not sure what to do. Should I bring the boxes to the house? Will that be a good thing or a painful one for Troy?"

Sympathy for his dilemma throbbed within her. She wished she had the answers he sought. She wasn't a child psychologist, and she didn't have experience with this kind of situation. She sent up a silent prayer for wisdom and guidance.

Placing a hand over David's heart, she said, "I can't tell you what the right thing to do is." She paused, a thought forming and taking hold. "I will say that I think it's important for you to keep Daniel and Beth's memory alive for Troy. The worst thing you could do is to pretend they didn't exist."

A stricken look crossed his face. "I've been doing that. I've been avoiding talking about Daniel because I don't want to cause Troy pain." He stepped back and ran a hand through his hair. "I'm not good at this. Why did they choose me?"

She grabbed his arm. "You are the perfect person for Troy. Don't doubt that. Daniel and Beth trusted you. I trust you."

He blinked. "You do?"

"I do." She knew this man would never deliberately hurt her

or Troy or anyone else. He was kind, compassionate. A man worth loving. Not that she did.

She wasn't ready to examine her feelings too closely. She might never be ready.

"Would you go with me tomorrow to retrieve the decorations? I don't want to overwhelm Troy by taking him there."

She knew it would be painful for him as well. And she wanted to be there to comfort him. She refused to analyze why that was. "Yes, of course I will."

He pulled her into his embrace. "Thank you. I don't know why, but God chose to bless me with you."

With her cheek laid against his beating heart, she closed her eyes and wondered how she was going to leave this man.

✳   ✳   ✳

The next morning, Sophie stood near the festively decorated Christmas tree with a cup of coffee in her hand and Riggs by her side. He had his paws on the window ledge, as if he knew they were expecting guests. Any second now David and Troy would arrive. Troy would be staying with Grandma, while Sophie accompanied David to the storage unit where he kept his brother and sister-in-law's belongings. Riggs barked just as Troy and David came into view.

Troy carried a Lego bucket with him. He was dressed in a long-sleeved T-shirt with Captain America's red, white, and blue shield on the front beneath a navy down vest. The bottoms of his jeans were rolled up at the ankles.

David had on a plaid flannel shirt and jeans. He'd shaved and looked ruggedly handsome.

Sophie's pulse sped at the sight of the two Murphy men. Affection filled her heart. She'd come to care for Troy and David in a way she'd never expected. Troy had carved out a special place in her heart. And David . . . well, she wasn't ready to think about how he'd affected her heart.

Troy ran up the porch stairs and banged on the front door. David followed him and waved at Sophie. She waved back and ignored the jolt of pleasure coursing through her.

Riggs jumped down to wait at the door.

"Okay, boy, back up," she said as she swung the door open.

Riggs pushed past Sophie to lick Troy's face, much to Troy's giggling delight.

A rush of emotion crashed through Sophie. Love. She loved this child. Her gaze strayed to David. The look of adoration on his face clutched at her heart.

Oh, no. Was she falling in love with David?

Not. Happening. The words rang hollow within her.

Grandma limped out of the kitchen without her crutches. The doctor had said she should begin to bear weight on her foot, so she had decided to try an ankle brace boot. "Good morning, you two. Troy, are you ready to play some games?" She pointed to the table where she'd stacked several board games.

"Yes." He held up the bucket of Legos. "I brought these to play with, too."

Grandma clapped her hands. "I love building cities and stuff. Should we do that first, or play Candyland?"

Troy ran to the table. "Candyland."

"We won't be long," David said to Grandma.

She smiled wide. "Take your time. Go do some shopping." She surreptitiously pointed to Troy. "Maybe you'll find something special."

"Good idea." Sophie gave a thumbs-up sign. They'd head to the toy section straightaway.

"Have lunch." Grandma winked. "Enjoy yourselves. Troy, Riggs, and I will be just fine."

Sophie knew Grandma suspected that her plan of setting up Sophie and David was working.

She jammed her arms into her jacket, grabbed her camera and purse, and then followed David to his truck. He'd put a hard cover over the bed to keep the back dry from the gently falling rain.

At the storage unit, he unlocked the padlock and then rolled up the door. The ten-by-ten space was filled with furniture and boxes stacked to the ceiling. "You weren't kidding when you said you put all of their belongings into storage."

"I didn't want to get rid of anything in case one day Troy wanted something," he said as he surveyed the contents of the unit. "Someday he'll have his own place and he might want the furniture."

The burgundy leather couch and love seat looked to be in good condition beneath the clear plastic wrapped around them. "He'll be set."

"The boxes are labeled." He pointed to her left. "You check over there. I'll take this side."

With a nod, she skirted around the couch to examine a stack of boxes. Her gaze snagged on a brightly colored toy box pushed against the back of the couch. Troy's, no doubt. She lifted the lid to find it full of toys. Some were too young for Troy now. She touched the head of a stuffed giraffe.

"Found them," David called out.

She lowered the lid and watched him carry a box marked *Christmas* to the truck. When he stepped back inside the unit, she gestured for him to come to her side. "Look at this."

He stared at the toy box. "I'd forgotten that was here."

"It would fit perfectly in Troy's bedroom." She thought of the corner where they'd pushed his toys.

"I don't know. He might get sad if I bring that home."

"Or he might be happy to see his old toys and remember the happy times," she countered.

He looked at her for a long moment and then turned away. He grabbed the second box of decorations and stowed it next to the other one in the truck bed. When he was done, he stood at the opening of the storage unit, his hand on the roll-down door. Waiting.

She sighed. She couldn't force him to take the toy box, nor could she make him be ready to deal with the memories it might evoke. Maybe in time he'd find the wherewithal to face the past. She exited the unit. David started to roll down the door, then stopped and dropped his forehead to the metal.

Sophie reached out a hand but halted as he let the door roll back up. Then he strode forward with purpose, picked up the toy box, and tucked it into the back of the truck beside the other boxes.

She smiled, pleased by his choice. He locked up the unit and then they drove to the mall. They spent the next few hours shopping, buying Troy new clothes and games and a bike.

"I know it will be months before he can ride it, but it seems like a good gift," David said.

"It's a great gift. He'll love it." She thought about suggesting a puppy, a certain Bernese mountain dog, but lately she'd begun to rethink finding Riggs a new home. Grandma was so fond of the dog and as long as she didn't try to step over him again, Riggs was a good companion. And it would be a good excuse for Troy and David to visit Grandma.

They ate in the restaurant of a high-end department store.

They had a nice window seat overlooking Bellevue. The Seattle suburban community, the fifth largest city in the state of Washington, had a skyline of gleaming high-rises against a stormy sky. Many of them were occupied by tech companies, like David's. "Can we see your office from here?"

"No, it's hidden behind that hotel." He pointed to a well-known hotel chain. "If you'd like, we can stop in there on our way out."

"I'd like to see your company, but if we stop there will you get roped in and feel the need to stay?"

He gave her a lopsided grin. "Maybe."

"How many times have you talked to the office today?"

"Six times."

"Six times and it's only noon?" She shook a finger at him. "Vacation, remember?"

"I'm trying to remember," he said. "Being here with you helps."

She picked up her iced tea and took a sip to hide the blush creeping up her neck.

He paid the check and they walked through the store.

"I'd like to buy your grandmother a gift but I'm not sure what would be appropriate," David told her.

She steered him toward the home accessory department. "She really could use a new throw blanket."

"I like that idea," he said and inspected the throws. He picked one in shades of blue that was soft and cozy. "This reminds me of Louise."

"It's perfect." Sophie would have picked it, too.

They made their way toward the exit when she saw the tie display in the men's section. "Uh, I'm going to use the ladies' room." She pushed her packages into his hands. "I'll meet you at the door."

She hurried away before he could offer to escort her. She wove her way out of his sight and then doubled back toward the ties, being as stealthy as she could. She glanced toward the spot where she'd left David, but he was gone. Maybe he was already waiting at the exit.

She thumbed through the silk ties until she found one that looked like something he'd wear, a navy tie with diagonal lines in a lighter shade of blue. She quickly bought it and rolled it up and stuffed it into her coat pocket, then made her way to the exit. Only David wasn't there. She waited another five minutes before he appeared around a corner.

At her quizzical look, he grinned. "Did a little shopping of my own."

"Ah." What did that mean? Had he seen her buy the tie? Or was he saying he'd bought her a gift? A pleased thrill danced through her as she took her packages and they headed to the parking garage.

As David pulled the truck out of the garage, he asked, "Home?"

"Your office?" she countered. She really was curious to see his work space. You could learn a lot about a person by their work environment. And with her there, he couldn't really get too caught up in anything.

David grinned. "I'd like to show you my company."

There was a hearty dose of pride in his tone. She was proud of him. It took a lot of perseverance and determination and grit to make a start-up company successful. More reasons for her to admire and respect this man.

He drove them to a high-rise tucked behind a thirty-floor hotel. He pulled the truck into a parking space beneath the building that had his name engraved on a plate attached to the wall.

They took the elevator to the tenth floor. The doors opened to a wide and open reception area with soft and comfortable seating arranged to foster intimate conversations. A flat-screen television mounted to the wall played a muted video of sea life, making Sophie want to sit and watch and experience swimming with dolphins in a tropical paradise. A polished mahogany reception desk with a large burgundy-colored vase filled with a bounty of beautiful exotic tropical flowers and leaves drew Sophie's eye.

Seated behind the desk, a stunning African American woman smiled in greeting. "David, we weren't expecting you today."

"Good afternoon, Eleanor. How are Mike and the kids?" David asked with warmth lacing his tone.

"They're well, thank you." She rose, revealing a height that nearly matched David's. She wore a vivid red dress with a scarf tied neatly about her neck that sported a Christmas motif. Her ebony skin was flawless and her dark hair, peppered with a few silver strands, was sleekly pulled back into a fashionable knot at her nape. "What a pleasant surprise to see you."

Her curious gaze made Sophie wonder if David brought many women into his office. Sophie noticed a framed photo on the credenza behind the receptionist. A studio portrait of the woman, with a handsome man and two preteens, one female, the other male. A happy-looking family.

"I hadn't planned to come in but we were out shopping nearby and I thought I'd show Sophie what we do here," David explained.

"Excellent," Eleanor replied.

"Sophie, this is my longtime receptionist Eleanor Mayfield. Eleanor, this is Sophie Griffith, my neighbor's granddaughter. She's been helping me with Troy."

Eleanor stuck out her hand. "Ah, so nice to meet you and thank you for helping out. We all appreciate it."

Sophie shook the woman's hand, noting her strong grip. "Nice to meet you, too. And it's been a pleasure to get to know Troy and David."

Eleanor centered her gaze on David. "Everything's running smoothly. Don't let the boys in the den tell you otherwise."

David chuckled. "I know I can always count on you to keep us all in line." He put his hand to the small of Sophie's back, the warm pressure sending little tingles up her spine. "This way. I'll give you the grand tour."

With one last smile at Eleanor, Sophie allowed David to lead her through an archway into a corridor. "This is a really nice space."

"When we moved in here two years ago I put a lot of thought into the aesthetics because it makes a difference with the clients," he replied. "We want to compete with the big dogs. The old space we had was in a strip mall. Not very appealing."

Glass walls separated the rooms on either side of the hall. The effect was very open and airy.

"This is the conference room," he said, stopping in the doorway of a large rectangular room. An oval conference table with comfortable captain chairs dominated the space.

Across the hall from the conference room was another office, and a blond-haired man in a suit sat on the phone. He waved as they passed.

"That's Ken Larson, my financial officer."

David urged her forward to an office door to the left. Blinds over the glass walls prevented her from seeing inside. A nameplate with letters engraved in gold read DAVID MURPHY. "My office."

He pushed open the unlocked door and stepped inside. She

followed him. The first thing she noticed was the wall of windows facing east. In the distance you could see the Cascade Mountains. Low cloud cover hid the tips of the mountains, but the view was spectacular.

The room itself was decorated in very masculine hues of browns and blues. A large cherrywood desk paired with an executive chair sat at an angle, giving David the advantage of seeing the door or the view outside. The desktop was neat and tidy with a desktop computer, a mugful of pens, and a letter holder. On the solid wall hung David's diplomas and a smattering of framed photographs. Sophie moved closer to inspect the images.

There was a photo of a white farmhouse with a wraparound porch and wheat fields in the background. Her heart squeezed tight. This must have been his family's farm. She turned to look at David. He regarded her with a small nod, as if he'd heard her thought.

The next photo showed three generations of Murphys on the same porch. David was a toddler, but even then he had a full head of dark hair. Another photo showed David as a teen with another young man—Daniel, she presumed. The two looked so much alike. The last photo showed Daniel, a smiling brunette with laughing dark eyes, and a baby dressed in a Christmas outfit. Sophie could see both Beth and Daniel in Troy's face.

"Come on, let's go see the guys," David said in a voice thick with emotion.

Sophie moved to him and put a hand on his arm. "This is lovely."

He covered her hand with his. "Thank you."

He tugged her out the door, pulling it closed behind him and led her to another open area, where several computer stations were set up with half a dozen men of various ages and ethnicities busily working. These men weren't dressed in suits and ties but rather in the comfortable, casual hipster style so popular these days with young men.

There were various-size tables and chairs scattered about. In the center of the space were beanbag chairs, couches, and large-screen consoles. On the outside walls were windows, allowing natural light to complement the overhead lights.

One of the men noticed them. "Hey, boss."

Sophie nearly laughed as the men jumped from their chairs and hustled over, each one staring at her and David with curiosity. David made introductions, but there was no way she'd ever remember their names and their titles. But the mutual admiration, respect, and affection between David and his employees were palpable.

"We could use some advice on the Tangerine," one young man said with eagerness. He had green eyes, red hair, and a goatee that matched.

David held up a hand. "Ethan, I'm on vacation, remember. Email me your questions and I'll get to them tonight."

As they left the building, Sophie tucked her arm around David's. "Email you their questions?"

He shrugged sheepishly.

She laughed. "Tangerine?"

"A software counting game for children," he replied. "We're building it on spec for a gameware company. They source out some of their work and we're glad to take it."

"You have a remarkable operation going here, David," she told him as she slid into the passenger seat of his truck.

"You're impressed?" he asked.

She heard a hint of insecurity in his voice. "Very much so."

He smiled, seeming satisfied with her announcement. She

wondered why he would question his value. The more she learned about this man the more she liked him. She liked his style. She liked his ethics. She liked how other people liked him. But mostly, she liked how he cared for the people important to him.

Guarding her heart from his appeal was becoming harder every moment.

* * *

When they arrived at his house, David parked the truck and then turned to Sophie. "Would you and Louise help us decorate our tree?"

She took his hand, her fingers lacing through his. "It would probably be better for you and Troy to unpack the memories together. Just family."

He knew she wasn't family. But she'd come to feel like it. She'd started to mean so much to him and Troy in such a short time. He wanted to argue with her and convince her to be there. He needed her support, her encouragement. He needed her in his life. She grounded him, made him feel like he could accomplish anything. She was the part of him that was missing.

Oh, man. That was exactly the reason he should accept her wise words. He'd told her no promises, no plans. Keep things between them fun and light. Needing her wasn't light. Needing her meant he was growing dependent on her. And that was the last thing he should be doing. He squeezed her hand. "You're right. This is something he and I need to do alone."

They headed next door so he could collect Troy. Sophie pulled up short at the foot of the porch stairs. "Uh, David."

He paused. "Yes?"

"The Christmas tree is gone."

He looked toward the front window. It was dark. "We can't see it because the Christmas tree lights aren't on."

"Maybe." But she didn't sound convinced.

Riggs barked a quick greeting as they entered. David bumped into Sophie in the entryway.

"Oh, no," she breathed out.

He peered around her to see the Christmas tree toppled on its side. Riggs was gnawing on the trunk like a chew toy. David clamped his lips together to keep from bursting into laughter. That dog was something else.

Sophie pointed to where Troy and Louise were snuggled on the couch beneath a threadbare afghan. Troy was asleep and Louise looked like she'd just awoken. *Rudolph the Red-Nosed Reindeer* played on the television, but the sound was muted.

"Grams, are you okay?" Sophie asked as she moved closer.

Louise smiled at them. "Of course. Did you have a good time? Get what you were after?"

"We did," David said as he came to a stop beside Sophie. "It looks like Riggs has had a good time too."

Confusion lit up Louise's eyes. Sophie stepped aside and gestured toward the fallen tree.

Louise gasped. "Oh, that scoundrel. I thought I heard something but I was so sleepy."

"We'll get the tree back in order," David assured her.

He and Sophie moved to the tree. Sophie shooed Riggs away from the now-chewed-up bottom part of the tree while David grasped the trunk in the middle and lifted the tree upright. He then replaced it in the tree stand. Sophie squeezed in next to him to hold the tree in place while he shimmied beneath to reattach the stand to the end.

When he crawled back out from under the tree, it only took

one look at the amused gleam in Sophie's eyes to know he was once again covered in pine needles. "I'll go shake off while you collect the downed ornaments."

She nodded and gathered the decorations. As far as he could tell, none had broken. When he returned from ridding himself of the needles, Sophie was sitting on the floor with Riggs's head in her lap. The dog was obviously trying to make up for his less-than-stellar behavior.

David scooped up Troy into his arms. "Thank you for watching him."

Louise stretched. "My pleasure."

Sophie jumped to her feet. "I'll follow you over and open the doors for you." She hurried ahead of him to hold the front door open.

Her thoughtfulness touched him. "I'd appreciate it."

They made their way to his house and went through the open garage door. Sophie hustled ahead of him to open the inner garage door.

"I'll say good-bye," she said in a hushed tone. "For now."

He liked that she added the "for now." He matched her hushed tone. "Do you and Louise have plans for tomorrow?"

"I don't think so."

"Would you care to join Troy and me ice-skating?"

Her eyes widened with delight. "I'd love to. I don't think Grandma would be much good on skates, but I bet she'd like to come along. Let's touch base in the morning."

He laughed, and she hurried away. With a pleased smile, he took Troy to his room and laid him on his bed. Troy curled onto his side.

David watched him for a long moment, then his gaze took in the pile of toys in the corner. Sophie had been right. The toy box would fit perfectly right there. Though he'd struggled to make the decision, he knew that listening to Sophie was the right choice.

Now if he could only get his heart to realize falling in love with her was the wrong choice.

❄   ❄   ❄

Two hours later, Troy wandered out of his room. David sat at his makeshift desk at the dining room table. He'd been able to get a lot of progress made on his app while Troy had slept. Now David set his work aside and picked Troy up. "I have a surprise for you. I hope you'll be okay with it."

"I like surprises," he said and hugged David.

David carried him to the living room, where he'd set the Christmas decorations and Troy's old toy box. He put Troy on his feet. The boy stared at the toy box for the longest time before tentatively opening the lid. With a squeal of delight, he grabbed a stuffed giraffe and tugged him free from the box. "Misawah."

"Me what's ah?" David's heart pounded with relief to see that Troy wasn't devastated, as he'd feared he'd be.

Troy held up the stuffed animal. "Me-saw-wah. Mommy bought him for me. He's named after the baby giraffe at the Woodland Zoo."

"Oh, well hello, Misawah."

Troy tucked the giraffe under his arm and dug through the box until he found an action figure from a superhero movie. "I'd wondered what happened to him." He shut the lid. "The rest are baby toys. I'm a big kid now."

David laughed and hugged him. "Yes, you are."

Troy moved to the boxes of ornaments. "Can we decorate the tree now?"

"Yes, we can."

David broke the tape on the boxes and peeled back the top flaps to reveal a colorful array of ornaments. Some were wrapped in tissue paper or bubble wrap.

Troy grabbed a molded plastic ornament in the shape of an ark with three baby animals on board. "This is my baby one." The side of the ark had the inscription BABY'S FIRST CHRISTMAS.

"That's very special."

Troy threaded a hook through the metal rung at the top of the decoration and then hung it on a low branch.

David lifted a bubble-wrapped package from the box. "What do you think this is?"

Troy knelt down and gently pulled the wrapping apart to reveal a delicate crystal angel tree topper.

"Mommy's angel," Troy breathed out in a tone of awe.

David took a bracing breath. "Let's put it on the top."

He lifted Troy up into his arms, then balanced him on his shoulder so he could reach the stubby knob at the apex of the tree. Then they stepped back to look at the pretty angel sparkling with the white lights strung along the branches.

"It's perfect," David said.

Troy slipped his arms around David's neck. "Mommy and Daddy are with the angels now."

Heart squeezing tight with emotion, David hugged Troy close and silently promised his brother he'd protect Troy with everything in him.

Troy squirmed to be set down. "There's more to put on."

"There sure is, buddy," David said, setting him on his feet. He picked up a miniature golf bag. "Your daddy loved to golf."

"Can we go golfing?" Troy took the ornament, put a hook on it, and nestled it on a branch.

"Come summer, we sure will." They'd both take lessons.

As they continued to pull out more decorations and talk about each one, David thought the only thing that would have made this time perfect would have been having Sophie there.

Best not to think like that, David told himself.

Fun and light. No promises, no plans. He needed to keep his focus on his priorities. Troy and his company. Sophie didn't fit into their future.

Yet, how was he going to survive when she left?

CHAPTER 13

"Those smell delicious." Sophie came into the kitchen, her mouth watering. Grandma stood at the electric grill with a spatula in her hand. Six large, round, fluffy pancakes were cooking. Morning's gray light flooded the house. Outside, the world was awash in customary Pacific Northwest rainy gloom, but Sophie's mood was buoyant. She'd slept well and anticipated a fun day with David and Troy.

Grandma smiled. "Would you mind warming up some syrup?"

"Of course." Sophie took the maple syrup jar from the refrigerator and poured a generous amount into a ramekin, then popped it in the microwave. "I'm waiting for David to call. He mentioned taking Troy ice-skating today. Would you like to join us?"

Grandma shook her head, then gave her a wide smile. "I have a date already."

"You do?" Sophie sat at the counter with her chin in her hand. "Do tell."

"Simon's taking me to the craft fair."

Was Grandma blushing? "I like Simon. And it's pretty obvious he adores you."

Grandma laughed softly. "He's nice. And he's definitely good for my ego."

"Did I mention that David took me to his office?"

Grandma paused. "No. And?"

Sophie told her about the place and the people. "I had no idea he was so successful."

"He's an impressive young man," Grandma stated.

"Yes. Yes, he is," Sophie agreed.

The microwave dinged just as Sophie's cell phone chimed with an incoming call. Excitement revved through her veins. David? She checked the caller ID and let out a deflated breath. Not David, but her agent. Dread crimped her chest. Had the magazine gig fallen through? She didn't want to answer and hear the bad news, but she hit the answer button anyway.

"Good morning," Sophie said.

"Hey, Soph, how are you? Still at your grandmother's in Seattle?"

"Bellevue, actually, and yes, I am. What's up?"

"So the skiwear company called—"

Sophie winced. Not good. "Okay. They decided to go with someone else?"

"What? Oh, no. They want to push the date up for the shoot. They want you in Zurich by the thirtieth."

"Of December?"

"Yep. Will that be a problem?"

Blowing out a breath, Sophie's shoulders drooped. *Yes, it will.* She had made plans with David to take Troy up the mountain to play in the snow between Christmas and New Year's. But if she didn't agree to arrive in Zurich earlier than planned, would the magazine go with another photographer? She wanted this job, didn't she? "I'll try to make it work."

"I can tell them you can't be there that soon," her agent said, but there was censure in her tone. "Only we run the risk of losing the job."

"I understand." Sophie had planned to head home to LA to change out her wardrobe, grab more of her equipment, and see the rest of her family before taking off. If she skipped seeing her family, she could fly in, hustle to her apartment, pick up what she needed, and then head straight back to the airport. She would be able to make the earlier date. She'd have at least half of the week with David and Troy. "I'll be there if I can leave LA on the twenty-ninth."

"Great," she said. "I'll let them know. I'll book your flight and send you the details. You may have to fly out on the twenty-eighth, but I'll see what I can do about the twenty-ninth. However, that won't give you much time to decompress before you have to jump into the work."

No, it wouldn't, but jet lag was a small price to pay to be able to hang out a few more days with David and Troy. "That's fine. Thanks."

"Yep. Talk to you soon." She clicked off.

Sophie set the phone aside as Grandma slid a plate with a small stack of pancakes in front of her.

"Everything okay?" Grandma asked. "You look a bit shell-shocked."

"That was my agent. The job that was scheduled for the first part of January has been moved up. They want me there at the end of this month."

"Oh." There was disappointment in Grandma's tone. "When do you leave?"

"They want me in Zurich, Switzerland, by the thirtieth." She picked up her fork, but her appetite had fled. "I'd have to head back to Los Angeles by the twenty-eighth or twenty-ninth."

"At least you can stay for Christmas." Grandma joined her at the counter. "We'd all be sad if you missed the Christmas Eve pageant."

"I'm not missing that for anything," she assured her. "And I'll be back."

"You will?" Grandma beamed. "That's fabulous news. When?"

Anxiety kicked up its heels inside her chest. Was she ready to commit to returning? "Sometime in the spring. Or summer."

There was no mistaking the subtle displeasure crossing Grandma's face. "I'll look forward to your next visit then."

Sophie's cell phone rang again, and this time it was David. Pleasure lifted her mood. "Hello."

"Hi, it's David," his deep voice said into her ear, sending a lovely shiver down her spine. Like she wouldn't recognize his voice. Or see his name on her screen.

"Good morning," she said. "Are we still on for ice-skating?"

"Yes. We're finishing up breakfast and then have a few things to do before we leave," he said. "Would you be ready to go in an hour?"

She glanced at the clock. It was nine now. "Sure, I'll be ready by ten."

"Great. I'm looking forward to seeing you," he said.

His words brought a thrilled rush of affection to fill her heart. "Me, too."

Sophie hung up and found Grandma watching her with speculation in her blue eyes. "What?"

"You're falling for him, aren't you? David, I mean."

"No, we're just friends." But the protest held no conviction. Uh-oh.

"Sophie, my dear, it's time for you to stop playing it safe."

She tucked in her chin. "I don't know what you mean." But she was afraid she did know.

"You spend your whole life looking through a lens. That way you don't have to actually experience the world. I worry that life will pass you by before you take a chance on letting love in." Grandma took her hand. "I've watched you with Troy and David. You light up when they are near. Yet you hide behind your camera, taking pictures, capturing so many moments from your time with them, with me, instead of really being present and in the moment."

Sophie's cheeks flamed. "That's not fair."

"Life is rarely fair." Grandma patted her hand. "I love that you've found joy in your work, but there's more to life than taking pictures."

She swallowed, but her throat wouldn't work. "I'm scared, Grandma," she admitted quietly. "I don't want to get hurt." She'd been down this road before and she'd discovered how quickly attraction fizzled out when reality settled in.

"I know, sweetie. But love means opening yourself up to risk." Grandma gave her a soft smile. "And it's worth it."

"Like you're doing with Simon?"

A tender expression touched Grandma's face. "Yes. Exactly."

Her grandma was so wise and strong. If she could be open to love again, couldn't Sophie open her heart to David?

Something deep inside spread through her, warming her blood and making her pulse jump. She'd fallen for David. She wanted to deny it, wanted to push the thought away and cling to the "friends only" label that they'd both put on their relationship. But lying to herself was never a good idea. She had to be honest. Yes, she'd fallen for David. Head over heels in love with a man who'd assured her he'd never ask her to stay. No plans, no promises.

It was so typical of her to want what she couldn't have.

She prayed God would mend her heart when the time came to leave. Because she'd be leaving a chunk of it behind.

❄   ❄   ❄

The ice rink was crowded with kids and adults of all ages. Small kids clung to their parents' hands. Teenagers whirled and twirled in the center of the large, oval rink. Sophie strapped on a pair of white rental skates, then helped Troy with his pint-size beige-colored skates. David had his own pair of black ice-hockey skates.

"You play hockey?" she asked, eyeing him as he stood still. He didn't wobble at all.

"I'd always wanted to play as a kid, but we couldn't afford it, so I joined a league a few years ago and learned how to skate as I learned to play. I needed an outlet," he said. "I don't get out on the ice as much as I used to these days. The more successful the company has grown the less time I have for outside activities."

She rose and balanced on the thin metal skate. Out in the lobby the floor was covered in rubber, but on the ice . . . she shivered. "I've only ice-skated a few times. I'm better on Rollerblades."

"It's the same principle," he told her. "Just find your balance and then go with it." He lifted Troy so he could get the skates under him. Holding Troy steady, David said, "Hang on to me, buddy. I won't let you fall."

They made their way to the gate that led to the ice. Sophie hung back as David positioned Troy in front of him and eased Troy onto the ice. Troy slipped and let out a surprised yelp but David held on, keeping the boy upright.

"Can you march like a toy soldier?" David asked Troy as he

demonstrated. Troy emulated David's movements. "Perfect. That's how you start. Just march."

Right. David made it look so easy. She edged out onto the ice next to them but clung to the railing that circled the rink. She tested the ice and her balance. David and Troy moved away from her, Troy marching as David used short, gliding strokes to propel them forward.

David glanced over his shoulder at her. "You good?"

She waved him on. "Peachy." What had she been thinking? She did as David had instructed Troy and marched, keeping a hand on the railing. Amazingly, she moved forward, sliding her hand on the railing for safety's sake. Soon she could march without holding on. She grew more confident in her balance and coordination. David and Troy did a full lap around the rink, then caught up with her on their second lap.

"Bend your leg and push off to stroke the ice," he instructed, and showed her and Troy both how to do it.

The move felt familiar. He was right; it was like Rollerblading. Soon she was gliding, progressing around the rink with David and Troy at her side. Round and round they went, keeping close to the wall and out of the way of the more advanced skaters. They occasionally had to veer from their path for young children or those who'd stopped for a break and clung to the railing along the wall. David showed them how to stop by thrusting their right foot forward at an angle.

The announcer came on, asking everyone to clear the ice for the Zamboni machine to resurface the top layer of the ice. Sophie followed David and Troy to the opening in the wall. She lost sight of them for a moment in the crush of people. Then a warm and strong hand captured hers. She found David at her side, Troy propped on his shoulder. "He wants to watch the Zamboni."

She nodded and squeezed closer to him, thankful for his steady presence and how right it felt when he encircled her waist with his arm. He steered them out of the crush to a place where Troy could still see the machine.

"That was fun," she told him with a smile. She expected him to release her, but he kept her close. Which was fine with her. As she listened to David explain what the big machine was doing, she sighed with contentment. How was she going to give this up? And for what? A job?

But it wasn't just a job. It was her career as a whole. It was what she'd spent her whole life working for. If she backed out of this job, she would get a reputation for being unreliable. She couldn't stay. This was her chance. This job was the first step to the career she'd always imagined. She wanted to earn her parents' respect, and to do that she needed to take the top job offers, go where the jobs took her.

Maybe she could come back here after the job in Zurich, she thought. But she knew it didn't work like that. If all went well in Zurich, she'd soon be off to some other exotic location. She could come back, but never for long.

How could she allow herself to fall in love knowing she'd always be leaving?

When the Zamboni left the ice, the announcer said it was time for the hokey-pokey. A cheer went up from the skaters and they flooded the rink.

"What's the hokey-pokey?" Troy asked.

David set him back on his feet. "A fun game. Come on, you two, let's hokey-pokey."

They skated to the center and squeezed into the oval circle of skaters as the music played. Sophie laughed as they showed Troy the moves.

"I don't think I can turn," Sophie cried as she shook her hands. She attempted a turn and ended up nearly doing a face plant.

David snaked an arm around her waist and tucked her close to his side. He held Troy with his other arm and they skated in a tight circle.

When the song ended, the skaters dispersed. David led Sophie and Troy back to the wall. "Good job on the hokey-pokey." He high-fived Troy, then Sophie.

She curled her fingers around his and held on. "Good job yourself."

They shared a moment, their eyes locking. He tugged her forward until their skates were touching. "You're beautiful."

Her heart stuttered at his words. "Thank you."

He grinned and then kissed her. A sweet, quick kiss, but it was enough to make her breath stall and her head swim. He released her and took off with Troy. She watched them make their way through the skaters. She loved them. Both of them. And hadn't the foggiest idea what to do about it.

❄   ❄   ❄

After a lunch break in the café attached to the ice rink, David couldn't wait to get back out on the ice. He'd forgotten how much he liked to skate. But even more, he liked watching the joy on Sophie's face as she mastered skating. She was doing so well. So was Troy. The kid was a natural. David decided formal lessons were in his nephew's future. Troy needed to be active and make some friends. He could join an ice-hockey team for youngsters. They could have a sport in common.

"Okay, everyone grab your sweetheart." The announcer's disembodied voice filled the rink. "It's couple skate." A love song played through the speakers.

Sophie turned to head for the break in the wall that led to the spectators' section.

"Where are you going?" David called out. "You're our sweetheart."

"Yeah," Troy piped up. "You're our sweetheart."

Sophie's cheeks brightened with a pretty blush and she skated back to them. She took Troy's hand and nodded with her chin for David to take Troy's other hand. David's heart flipped over as he grasped Troy's hand. With Troy between them, they skated together, like a real family.

He couldn't help the tidal wave of longing that hit him square in the chest. He wanted this. Wanted to make a family with Sophie. He'd fallen in love with her. The thought wound a corded rope of apprehension and fear around his chest. She was leaving, he reminded himself.

He'd promised he wouldn't ask her to stay. He couldn't. It wouldn't be fair. He couldn't ask her to give up her dream job, an opportunity to further her career. Not when he knew once this vacation was over and life returned to its new normal, David would have to refocus all his energy into his company when he wasn't with Troy. There wouldn't be anything left for a romance.

Was that true? Or was he afraid?

The unbidden questions made his mouth go dry. Of course he was afraid. Pain always followed love. Yet he had a hard time equating Sophie with pain. She was light and good and everything that a man could want in a wife.

Oh, man.

He wasn't looking for a wife. Didn't want that kind of emotional turmoil.

But Daniel and Beth had been happy. Their parents had been happy.

As long as we're together, his mom would say, life can throw anything it wants at us.

And it had. Painful, horrible things.

Things that were out of their control.

The disturbing thoughts twirled around his mind like the skaters on the ice.

On their second lap around, Troy drew their hands together until David was holding Sophie's. "You two go round," Troy urged and then he skated to the side.

"He and Grandma must be in cahoots," Sophie said with a laugh as she skated next to him.

"Cahoots?" He liked holding her hand, their gliding steps in sync.

"In case you haven't noticed, Grandma has been playing matchmaker."

He wagged his eyebrows. "Oh, I've noticed."

And he was helpless to stop it. Didn't want to, in fact. Which left him confused and conflicted. Especially when her shy smile caused his heart to twist like a pretzel in his chest. How could he be so happy with her yet resist looking forward to a future together?

He'd never been in a situation like this before and wasn't sure what to do.

When the song ended and the announcer called out, "All skate to the last song of the public session," David and Sophie returned to Troy's side.

"Okay, buddy, this is the last time around," David told Troy, though he had to admit he was enjoying the skating so much more with Sophie at his side.

"Why?" Troy groused as they moved out onto the ice.

"It's the way it works, kiddo," Sophie said. "I saw on the schedule they have a figure-skating class after this."

"I don't want to go home," Troy muttered and jerked away from David.

David's stomach clenched. Oh, no. Please, Lord, not a tantrum here on the ice.

Troy pulled ahead of them, his little legs digging into the ice and his arms pumping. Concerned that Troy would fall or cause someone else to fall, David shot Sophie a quick glance and saw her nod; then he took off at a fast pace after Troy.

Troy cut away from the wall and headed toward the center of the rink, where a group of older teens was skating backward and spinning around each other.

"Troy, no!" David called out.

Troy didn't stop, but forged headlong into the group. A large teen spun on his skates, not noticing Troy until it was too late. The teen struggled to stop but he rammed into Troy with his hip, sending them both flying. Troy's feet came out from beneath him and he landed on his back, his head hitting the ice, hard.

It seemed as if the world froze. David could no longer hear the music. Only the roar of panic filling his veins.

"Troy!" David's heart stopped. He skated to Troy's side. Troy's eyes were closed. Red seeped onto the ice. David couldn't breathe as panic gripped him in a stranglehold. "Please, Lord, no." His first instinct was to gather Troy into his arms. He reached for him.

"Don't touch him," came a stern voice. A man in a red jacket with a white cross on the breast pocket knelt beside Troy. "I'm the ice marshal. Let me get this on him. Then we'll lift him onto the litter." The man gingerly placed a neck collar around Troy's neck.

David blinked as the world resumed and the noise of the rink returned. Soft hands clutched his arm. He turned to find Sophie next him, her face pale and her eyes large and worried.

"Help me lift him," the ice marshal said.

David gathered Troy's torso while the ice marshal gently lifted his head. The boy that had slammed into Troy lifted Troy's feet. They secured him onto the litter.

"An ambulance is on its way," someone said from behind them.

The ice marshal lifted a rope attached to the litter and then skated toward the gate, dragging the litter behind him. David and Sophie hurried after him.

By the time they had the litter at the front lobby, the ambulance had arrived. The paramedics took possession of the litter and Troy. They assessed him, then lifted the litter into the back of the ambulance. David handed Sophie the keys to his truck before he climbed into the ambulance next to Troy.

One paramedic shot a sharp glance at the skates still on David's feet. David didn't flinch. The paramedic shrugged and closed the doors.

Through the little windows cut out in the back doors of the rig, David saw Sophie standing on the sidewalk as the ambulance pulled away. When she was out of sight, he took Troy's hand and bowed his head.

"Lord, I know I have no right to ask, but please . . . I can't lose him."

At the hospital, David was forced to stay back as the nurses and orderlies rushed in to take Troy out of the ambulance. Then they whisked Troy to the emergency room. David followed, the skates on his feet clicking on the hospital floor, but a nurse blocked the way as the doors swung shut behind Troy.

"Sir, you can't go back there," the nurse said.

"But my son," David said. "He needs me."

"He's getting the best care possible." She steered him toward a desk. "We need you to fill out some forms."

"Forms?" Forms weren't important. All that was important was Troy. Tears burned the backs of David's eyes.

The nurse gently pushed him into a chair at a desk. The woman sitting on the other side stared at him with compassion. David had no idea what the forms said or what he signed. He couldn't think, couldn't process. Where was Sophie?

Then she was there. Her touch tender, her heart in her eyes. She was his anchor in the stormy chaos of panic and fear. He reached for her, like a lifeline. And froze.

Alarm bells clanged loudly inside his head. What was he doing? Lifelines could be severed. Cut clean through by drought and disease. In car crashes and freak accidents. The only control he had was protecting himself and Troy. He jerked back and stared at the floor.

He'd vowed he'd never risk his heart or be this vulnerable to anyone. But he'd never been this raw, this exposed in his life. He needed to lock his emotions down and refocus his energy on keeping Troy safe and his business thriving. He couldn't make room for anything else. Anyone else.

CHAPTER 14

Sophie sat on a hardback chair in the ER waiting area and stared at David in confusion and hurt. When she'd finally reached his side with his shoes in hand, she was sure she'd seen relief in his eyes at her arrival. But then the next second he'd withdrawn, shut down, locked her out.

Now he had his hands jammed into the pockets of his coat, his head bowed. He paced the length of the emergency room lobby as they waited for the doctors to give them an update on Troy.

Her heart beat too fast in her chest and she struggled to regulate her breathing. The frantic drive to the hospital had stretched her already overburdened nerves. She'd wanted to run red lights to keep up with the ambulance but had forced herself to remain in possession of her judgment.

It wouldn't have helped if she'd caused an accident. It was bad enough that Troy had fallen on the ice, hitting his head.

From the looks of it, he'd split open his scalp. She'd seen her brothers' head wounds growing up and knew that the scalp bled easily. There was no way to tell by the amount of blood on the ice how bad the cut was. But that wasn't what worried her. The fact that he'd lost consciousness was what had her stomach in knots.

At the very least, he'd have a concussion, but it could be worse. She'd prayed the whole way to the hospital for Troy to wake up and that there'd be no lasting damage.

"Sophie? David?"

Grandma and Simon approached. Simon had a steadying arm around Grandma's waist as she hobbled in on her booted foot.

Sophie jumped up to rush into her grandma's waiting arms. She'd called Grandma the second she'd parked in the hospital parking garage. Thankfully, Grandma and Simon had been headed home from the craft fair.

"How is Troy?" Grandma hugged her tightly.

Simon patted her back. The tender gesture brought tears to Sophie's eyes.

"We don't know yet." Sophie stepped back, trying to gather her control. "Thank you for coming."

"Of course." Grandma eased herself onto a chair. "Tell me what happened."

Sophie sank down beside Grandma and told her and Simon about their day at the skating rink. "I should have anticipated he wouldn't cooperate."

"He's not your responsibility," David said in a low tone as he halted in front of them. "*I* should have known. *I* should have handled the situation differently. This is *my* fault."

Sophie's heart thudded with a dull ache. David blamed himself. "Oh, David."

"No one is to blame," Grandma cut in crisply. "It was an accident. Troy will learn to control himself as he matures. But life happens. We all act impulsively at times, and nothing is guaranteed."

David's hooded gaze hid his thoughts. His jaw tightened and he resumed pacing. Sophie itched to wrap her arms around him and comfort him. That's what families did for each other in crisis. But from the stiffness in his shoulders and the harsh lines on his face, she doubted comforting was what he wanted.

The waiting seemed interminable.

"Would anyone like some coffee?" Simon asked.

Sophie shook her head.

David didn't respond.

Grandma put her hand on Simon's arm. "Thank you, but no. I don't think I could stomach it."

Simon nodded. Sophie felt bad for him. He hadn't asked to be stuck in the ER lobby with them. "If you need to leave, Simon, I can take Grandma home."

Simon arched an eyebrow. "I'm right where I need to be."

If Sophie weren't so concerned about Troy, she'd have sighed with delight at Simon's obvious devotion to her grandmother.

David stopped. "What's taking so long?"

Though Sophie knew the question was directed at no one in particular, she rose and went to his side. "I'm sure the doctor will come out soon."

David's steel gray gaze raked over her and then away. He walked to the window overlooking the parking lot. "I hope so. This waiting is driving me crazy."

"David." Simon drew their attention. "Louise mentioned you're working on an app that will change the world. How is that coming along?"

Slowly David turned from the window. "You told your grandmother?"

Sophie drew her chin back. An anxious tremor rumbled in her gut. "Not the details. Just that you were working from home."

He raked a hand through his hair. "I asked you to keep that to yourself."

She put a hand on his arm. "I didn't reveal anything crucial."

David turned away, but not before she glimpsed the disappointment in his eyes. "It's fine. In the grand scheme of things it doesn't matter."

But it did matter. He mattered to her. Didn't he know that? Maybe she shouldn't have mentioned the app, but she honestly hadn't thought he'd be upset about Grandma knowing why he was working from home.

"Mr. Murphy?" A dark-haired man wearing a white lab coat and a stethoscope around his neck approached.

David practically pounced on the doctor. "Troy?"

"I'm Dr. Kakar," the man stated. "Troy is your son?"

"Nephew. I'm his guardian," came David's tense reply. "How is he?"

The doctor's calm smile included them all. "He's awake and in good spirits. Quite talkative. His scalp required two sutures but the wound won't leave a scar."

Sophie sagged in relief to hear Troy was okay.

"Thank you, God," Grandma murmured and hugged Simon.

David's tension visibly drained. Suddenly he looked haggard and worn. "Can I go to him?"

"A nurse is with him," Dr. Kakar said. "I have at-home instructions for you. Mostly he'll need to rest for the next few days. If he complains of a headache, or double vision, please call ASAP. I'd like you to follow up with his pediatrician."

"I will," David promised. "Now may I see him?"

"Right this way," the doctor said and turned.

Sophie rose, wondering if she should follow David, but he took off without a backward glance, leaving her feeling as if she stood on shifting sand. Watching his retreating back, she had the same choking sensation she'd experienced as a kid when her brothers would leave her behind, as if she didn't matter.

"Go with him," Grandma urged. "He's hurting and scared and confused. He needs you. Even if he doesn't realize it."

And I need him, Sophie thought. Talk about scared. But right now wasn't about her. She had to put her own fears and old hurts aside to do what she could to support David and Troy.

She hurried to catch up with David. When he glanced at her, his eyes widened. For a moment there was a softening, then the steel gray flattened and he turned away to follow the doctor into a room. If he needed her, as Grams said, he was doing a good job of fighting it. She lowered her chin and matched his stride. She'd show him *fight*.

Troy's happy chatter greeted them. He was regaling the nurse with a story about Riggs. Sophie's heart squeezed tightly. Love spread through her. She had to check herself to keep from rushing to Troy's bedside and scooping him into her arms. Instead, she hung back as David did exactly what she wanted to do.

David gathered Troy close. "Kid, you are going to shorten my life span."

"Look, Uncle David!" Troy wormed his arm free and pointed to his head. "I've got stitches."

"That's what I heard," David murmured. He closed his eyes.

Sophie couldn't stop herself from inching closer, desperate to be included in their reunion.

"Initially you'll keep them dry and then you'll need to keep the wound site clean," Dr. Kakar said. "We'll give you supplies along with written instructions."

"I don't have to take a bath!"

Sophie couldn't help a laugh from escaping. "Maybe still take a bath, just not wash your hair."

Troy spied her and beamed. "Sophie!"

David's spine straightened. He slowly released Troy. "Sophie was worried, too. She came to make sure you were okay."

Taking David's words as an invitation, she closed the distance and laid a hand on Troy's leg. "I'm happy to see you."

David edged away from her and spoke to the doctor. "Can I take him home now?"

Dr. Kakar nodded. "Yes. I'll get the discharge papers ready." He looked to Troy. "Troy, stay on your feet from now on, okay?"

Troy gave the doctor the thumbs-up sign. "Yes, sir."

"Let's get Troy into a wheelchair," the nurse said. "Hospital policy."

David stepped back to the bed. "Excuse me," he said to Sophie.

His politeness grated on her nerves. She moved out of his way so he could lift Troy and place him in the wheelchair the nurse brought in. As they waited for the discharge papers, David said, "Do you mind catching a ride home with your grandma and Simon?"

Sophie's heart stalled as hurt and rejection tumbled through her. "Okay. I can do that."

He gave a decisive nod, then turned his attention to the doctor returning with the papers for him to sign.

She didn't understand what was happening. Why was he pushing her away?

David wheeled Troy to the lobby, where Grandma and Simon gushed over Troy. When David held out his hand for the keys to his truck, her shoulders drooped. He was serious about not riding home together.

She fished his keys out of her purse and handed them over. "It's on the top level in the second row near the elevator."

"Thank you." He briefly met her gaze. The flinty expression there left her cold.

"Louise, Simon, thank you for coming. Sophie will be riding home with you." With that, he pushed Troy out of the hospital. Why did it feel like he was pushing his way out of her life, too?

❋　❋　❋

"Uncle David, I'm bored," Troy whined from the couch where he lay with a blanket and pillow. The doctor had advised no television as well as rest. So David had set his music player up in the living room and had downloaded a mix of children's songs for Troy to enjoy. "Can't I go next door and see Sophie and play with Riggs?"

David gritted his teeth against the request, as he had every time Troy had made the same plea over the past two days. David had hedged over and over again, saying the doctor's orders had been to lay low, which meant no playing and no roughhousing, as Troy and Riggs would no doubt do.

It hadn't helped that Sophie texted repeatedly, asking about Troy, and Louise had called. They'd asked to visit but he'd put them off with the same excuse.

There was no way for David to explain to his five-year-old nephew the complicated reasons why it was best to steer clear of the Griffith women, particularly Sophie. He couldn't tell Troy that he'd fallen in love with Sophie and somewhere along the way had allowed her to become so deeply ingrained in his heart that he felt like he couldn't function without her. Troy was too young to understand why David had to excise her from their lives. Their hearts.

He was so mad at himself for going down this road. He knew

better than to let anyone in. Knew the danger of opening up his heart and life. And now not only was he paying the price, but so was Troy.

There was no rational reason why David had fallen for Sophie. No rational reason why he'd let her slip under his defenses. It didn't make sense. Life hadn't made sense for a while now. Would it ever again?

David hoped so once the ache of loss eased. He rose from his makeshift desk and came to sit beside Troy on the couch. "I know you want to see Louise and Riggs. You will see them again when you're better. You have to be patient. You took a hard knock on the noggin."

"But I *am* better," Troy said, sitting up. "I want to play with Riggs."

"You will see him tomorrow. Christmas Eve, remember?" David's stomach knotted. They'd also see Sophie. Her pretty blue eyes and sweet smile flashed through his mind. He pushed the image away. "You can hang on until then, can't you?"

Troy sighed. "I'll try."

David swallowed, not at all confident that trying would translate into waiting, but for now he'd take it. "Thanks, buddy."

They just needed to get through the holiday. Then he was going to take Troy away for the rest of Sophie's visit. That way, when she left, they'd already be far away.

❄️   ❄️   ❄️

Riggs had his paws on the front windowsill, his hot breath fogging up the window as he stared out at the soggy midafternoon. He let out a mournful whimper. Sophie tangled her fingers in his fur and heaved a sigh of her own. They missed Troy and David.

The scent of brownies wafted in the air. Grandma had decided to make more treats for tomorrow's Christmas party at the church. Normally the smell would have Sophie's mouth watering, but she was too upset to be hungry for chocolate. That was telling.

She'd taken Riggs for a walk twice today. Three times yesterday. Each time they'd gone past David's house, hoping he or Troy would see them and come out or invite them in, but no go. The front curtain had been closed for the past two days, and David's short replies to her text messages weren't encouraging.

Only concern that she would disturb Troy if he were resting had kept her from banging on the front door. For whatever reason, he'd decided to be done with her. Apparently Grandma was wrong. David didn't need her. The ache deep in her heart pulsated anew.

It was just as well, right? She wasn't ready to settle down. She wasn't ready to give up her transient lifestyle for home and hearth, despite the freshly reawakened yearning that beckoned to her.

Chalking David up to another failed relationship, one that hadn't even gotten off the ground, she turned away from the window and went back to her computer at the dining room table. She was making a digital photo album for David of the past ten days. She'd email it to him when she was done. And would give the Murphy boys their physical gifts tomorrow at the church's Christmas party. She heaved another sigh.

"What's wrong?" Grandma stood in the doorway between the kitchen and the dining room.

Sophie planned to hedge, but when she opened her mouth, she said, "I miss him."

Grandma raised her eyebrows. "Troy?"

A wry smile lifted the corners of Sophie's mouth. "Yes, Troy, too."

"Ah." Grandma hobbled to the table. She sat next to Sophie. "Have you told David you love him?"

Sophie swallowed back the panic the question caused. She did love David. There was no use in denying it. As much as she wanted to hide from the truth, she couldn't. "No, I haven't told him. He doesn't seem to want to see me. And he was so distant at the hospital, like I was in the way."

Her shoulders sagged. Her chest throbbed with loss. She wasn't sure why she hurt so much. She'd been through breakups before, but this agony was core deep and spreading through her with long tentacles of pain.

Grandma took her hand. "He's trying to figure out how to cope with everything. Seeing Troy fall on the ice was a shock. This was the first real accident David had to deal with since he lost his brother and sister-in-law. But I can guarantee it won't be his last. Your father was always getting banged up as a kid and teen. Your brothers, too, if you remember."

Sophie did remember multiple trips to the ER with one brother or another over the years. She'd even gone fairly recently when her oldest brother had wiped out on his motorcycle. That had been frightening for them all. "David wouldn't let me help him deal with his pain. I was right there. I wanted to comfort and support him but he shut me out."

Grandma tilted her head, her gaze assessing. "He knows you're leaving, right?"

Sophie nodded. Her stomach knotted.

"I would imagine he's protecting himself from needing to lean on you when he knows you're only in his and Troy's life temporarily." Grandma patted her hand. Her sad eyes bore into Sophie. "I think it's time you decide what you truly want in *your* life." With that she rose and made her way back to the kitchen.

Grandma's words shot straight through Sophie's heart. Grandma was right. Thinking back to the hospital, Sophie had recognized what David was doing. He was fighting his need for her. But she should have realized it was because he mistakenly felt that he could only rely on himself and not others. Considering all that he'd shared with her about his past, it made so much sense, yet was so erroneous.

They were stronger together than apart.

The realization slammed into her chest like an iron fist.

She knew what she wanted in life. With a few keystrokes she brought up a photo taken the night of the Snowflake parade. It was a shot of her, David, and Troy. Simon had asked to use her camera, and he'd captured them together, looking like a family. Her family.

She wanted David and Troy. She wanted to be a part of their world more than she wanted to see the world. She wasn't going to let him push her away. She was going to fight for what she wanted. And she wanted David. She would find a way to make it work. She sent up a prayer that he'd want her, too.

"Sophie!" Grandma called from the kitchen. "Come here!"

Sophie's heart jumped, praying Grandma hadn't fallen again or hurt herself somehow. Sophie hurried to the kitchen, where Grandma stood at the sink. "Are you okay?"

Grandma pointed out the window. "We have a visitor."

Sophie didn't see anything. "I don't—"

Riggs barked and raced for the back door. He scratched to be let out. Curious, Sophie went to the door and let the dog out. He raced across the back patio to the darkened far corner. Sophie followed and could just barely make out a little boy hiding under a wheelbarrow. Affection and love for this child crowded her chest.

"Troy, come out of there," Sophie said. "What are you doing?"

Troy climbed out. He was covered in dirt from the damp soil. "I wanted to see you but then I was afraid I'd get in trouble."

With a sinking feeling, Sophie squatted down to the boy's eye level. "Did you run away again?"

Troy nodded. "I was bored and I wanted to see Riggs."

At the sound of his name, the dog let out a happy bark. He nudged Troy with his nose, and the boy flung his arms around Riggs's neck and buried his face in the thick fur.

"Oh, boy." Sophie sighed. She had to tell David. He was probably out searching the neighborhood, frantic with worry and berating himself again. The man took on responsibility for things that weren't within his control. "Come on, kiddo. Let's go find your uncle."

"Can Riggs come, too?"

"Of course," she said with a laugh. "Let's get his leash."

After leashing up, they headed next door. Sure enough, David wasn't there. The door was open, as if he'd run out without giving any thought to locking up. She pulled the door closed and called David's cell.

A moment later, he answered, his voice edged with panic. "Sophie, Troy ran away again. I'm at the park but I can't find him."

"David, he's here," she told him. "Come to my grandma's."

A long moment of silence stretched. "I should have guessed. I'll be right there." He clicked off.

Sophie led Troy and Riggs back to the warmth of Grandma's house. Grandma had made hot chocolate and set out a plate of cookies. She leveled Sophie with a pointed look. "You and David need to talk."

"I know," she said, a battalion of nervous butterflies taking flight in her stomach. What if she confessed her love to him and he rejected her? She squared her shoulders. She'd deal with it. Better to get it out in the open than to keep it bottled up inside.

A knock sounded at the door. Taking a deep breath, Sophie opened the door. David stood there, looking so handsome and worried. His jeans and white T-shirt had grown damp from the misty air. Goose bumps covered his bare arms. At least he had on shoes, but they were wet and muddy. His dark hair was brushed back, like he'd been running his fingers through the strands, something she noticed he did when nervous or upset. As their gazes locked, she saw a hint of longing just beyond the anxiety in his eyes.

It took everything in her not to wrap her arms around him. She needed him to see that Troy was safe first. She stepped aside so David could enter. He slipped off his shoes, leaving them by the front door. He stared at Troy, who sat in front of the fireplace munching on a cookie with Riggs by his side.

David ran a hand through his disheveled hair. Relief bowed his shoulders. "That boy is going to be the death of me."

Sophie chuckled. "My dad used to say the same thing about Dean. He was a daredevil and so impulsive. But he turned out well."

He slanted her a quick glance. "Thanks again."

She captured his hand. "We need to have a chat."

He pressed his lips together and extracted his hand. "No. What I need to do is get Troy home and bathed. He's a mess and getting your carpet dirty."

"David." Sophie wanted to shake him. She wanted to pull him in close and tell him he didn't have to go it alone.

But he moved past her and knelt down beside Troy. "It's time to go home, Troy. Please say good night to the ladies and Riggs."

Troy kept his head down. His little hand shook as he set a cookie back on the plate.

When he didn't respond, David lifted his chin with the crook of his finger. "Now, please."

Troy sighed, bounced to his feet, and did as David asked without protest.

"Good night. We'll see you tomorrow for the Christmas pageant," Troy said and shuffled his feet toward the door. David strode after him.

A deep sadness welled within Sophie. She hated this distance between her and David. But she didn't know how to breach it. Fighting for what she wanted was foreign territory.

But if he wouldn't even talk to her, then how could she ever hope they could find their way back to the place they were before Troy's accident? A place where she could tell him she loved him?

CHAPTER 15

Christmas Eve arrived with a cold front that blasted an icy rain through the city. Flecks of ice hit the front windshield of David's truck like a million little fingers tapping at the glass as he pulled into a parking spot in front of the Good Hope Christian Church.

He flexed his fingers on the steering wheel. His nerves jumped. He really didn't want to go inside. Not only because he'd have to confront a scene that would bring back all the memories of his childhood, but also because he'd have to face Sophie. Dear, sweet Sophie.

He'd awoken this morning to find a digital photo album in his in-box. A Christmas gift from Sophie.

It had broken his heart to see the happy and carefree images on the screen. The day Troy had run away to the park. The muddy mess he, Troy, and Riggs had been. Pictures from their Christmas tree hunt. The parade. He hadn't realized she'd captured Troy hugging Olaf.

One photo in particular had brought the burn of tears to his eyes. The one of the three of them taken at Ferralla's restaurant. The joy shining in Sophie's eyes, the silly grin on his own face, and Troy's delighted expression. They looked like a happy family.

He'd stared at the picture filling his computer screen for a long time before he finally shut the computer off. He didn't think he'd ever be able to look at the photo again. Because he loved Sophie, wanted her in his life. But he was too afraid to let her in.

An image of her face so sad yesterday tormented his mind. He'd missed her so much these past few days. And seeing her yesterday had nearly crumbled his resolve to keep her out of his life.

There was no hope of keeping her out of his heart. She was already there, taking up way too much space, but he had to figure out how to live without her. She'd said yesterday they needed to talk. He didn't want to go there because he knew he'd break down and tell her he loved her and ask her to stay. That was one thing he'd promised he wouldn't do. The one thing guaranteed to put his heart at risk.

If she didn't feel the same, then he'd feel the sting of rejection. But if she did feel the same, then everything would change. There would be no safety net to catch him if anything were to happen and she left or was taken away from him.

Just the thought of it made him break out in a cold sweat.

He heard the click of Troy undoing the buckles on his car seat.

"Come on, Uncle David," Troy said as he pushed his way between the two front captain's seats. "Let's go in."

David ruffled Troy's hair. "Impatient much?"

"Yes." Troy grinned.

David laughed and scanned the parking lot. Kids and parents climbed from various cars and hurried toward the entrance. He didn't see Sophie's rental car. She'd most likely parked in the back of the church. David popped open his door and stepped out of the truck. He held out his arms for Troy to jump into.

"Wait!" Troy said. "What about Sophie and Grandma Louise's presents?"

The bag with the gifts they'd wrapped was tucked behind the driver's seat, out of view. "We'll give the ladies their gifts after the pageant."

Troy seemed to accept that announcement.

He pushed on David's arms, asking to be set down. David set him on his feet but grabbed his hand to keep him from running through the parking lot.

They entered the church through the main doors and followed the throng of people to the great room. The happy sounds of children's laughter filled the air. As David and Troy stepped into the room, Troy broke free from David's grasp and raced across the room. Sophie sat at a table with several little girls and a few teenage girls making some sort of craft. She opened her arms to Troy and hugged him tightly.

A pang of yearning struck David. His gaze never left Sophie as she rose, grabbed her camera from the chair next to her, and hand in hand with Troy, made her way toward him.

She had on a bright red sweater decorated with white snowflakes and black pants tucked into tall black boots. Her blond hair hung loose about her shoulders and was sprinkled with green glitter. Her eyes sparkled like sapphires. She had a dusting of gold glitter on her cheeks. She'd never looked more beautiful to him.

She stopped in front of him. "I'm glad you two are here."

His heart thumped. "You are?"

Her smile was soft and full of something close to love that tied his insides in knots. "Yes." She turned to Troy. "Grandma is over there. She'd love to see you."

Troy turned to race to where Louise, Simon, and Riggs sat along the wall with several other couples their age. Riggs's tail thumped on the floor as little kids took turns petting him. Simon whispered something in Louise's ear and she blushed, but her smile lit up her face. Then she was hugging Troy like he really was her grandson. Louise waved, and David raised a hand in greeting.

"This is quite the crowd." He turned his gaze back to the room. To the melee of children of all ages, some playing games, others doing crafts or taking snacks from the tables laden down with Christmas goodies.

"It's a good turnout."

He took an envelope from the inside pocket of his sport coat and handed it to her. "Here, before I forget." *Or lose my nerve.*

Her gaze narrowed. "That better not be a check. I told you, you don't owe me anything for watching Troy."

He pressed the envelope into her hand. "Just take it, please. Don't open it here. Wait until later." *Like on the plane to Zurich.*

He could see she wanted to argue with him. "Please."

With a sigh, she nodded and tucked it into the back pocket of her pants. "We need to talk, David. Soon."

His mouth went dry. "Sure. Later." *Like never.* He folded his arms across his chest.

She arched an eyebrow as if she'd heard his thought.

Pastor Jeff halted beside them. "Hello, David."

"Jeff." David shook the other man's hand.

"Do you mind if I steal Sophie from you?" Jeff said. "The craft girls are in need of some guidance."

Yes. No. David's stomach churned. "Sure."

"I'll be right over," Sophie told the pastor. Once Jeff moved away, she put her hand on David's folded arms. "When you look around here, what do you see?"

He frowned. "Kids. Food. Presents."

"Look deeper, past the obvious." She leaned in and kissed his cheek. He automatically unfolded his arms to allow her closer, to reach for her, but she was already stepping away. "You might be surprised."

With that cryptic remark, her kiss imprinted on his cheek, she walked away and joined the girls at the craft table. What did she mean, "look deeper"?

His gaze scanned the room, taking in the happy faces of the children, the parents talking to each other. He had to admit it was a festive party. Everyone seemed to be having a good time. He felt out of place, like an outsider looking in. A familiar feeling. He refolded his arms across his chest. He couldn't help it.

Then his gaze snagged on a boy in the far corner of the room. David guessed the kid was about eleven or twelve. His posture mirrored David's.

The kid leaned against the wall with his arms folded over his thin chest and had a scowl on his face. David recognized the resentment in the kid's eyes. David had felt the same way so many years ago, every time his parents would drag him to events exactly like this one.

No doubt the preteen begrudged the free gifts and food, and the pity that he figured everyone felt for him. But David didn't sense any pity in this gathering.

Only a generous spirit of love and hope.

His gaze sought Sophie's. The knowing look in her eyes said she'd seen him notice the kid. She nodded with a smile, encouraging him to take a chance.

Slowly, David unfolded his arms and shook them out at his sides. He rolled his shoulders and waded in.

❋   ❋   ❋

"Here you go, sweetie." Sophie handed a cookie to a little girl who was about three. Her chubby hands grasped the treat and she rewarded Sophie with a grin.

The party was winding down. Pastor Jeff was encouraging everyone to make their way to the sanctuary for the Christmas Eve pageant. After a quick rehearsal, Troy and the other children in the pageant returned, and had been building Legos together ever since. Now they were picking up the pieces and dumping them back into buckets.

Riggs loved all the attention from the kids and adults alike. Even Grandma and Simon had made some crafts at the craft table. Everyone had had a good time.

Even David. She sighed with love and affection for the man. She was so proud of him. She'd been watching him when his gaze landed on the preteen boy in the corner. The kid held himself apart from everyone else. Sophie's heart ached as she envisioned David as a young teen in the kid's place.

David made his way across the room to the boy. She'd strained to discern what they were talking about, but she was too far away. When David walked away to settle at the board game table alone, she'd despaired for the young man. Had David given up on him?

David set up a chess game and waited. After several long min-utes, the preteen pushed away from the wall and slowly joined David, sitting across from him with the chessboard between them. They'd been embroiled in a game ever since.

"Is he your husband?" A woman moved to Sophie's side.

Sophie blinked. "Who?" She followed her gaze back to David. "Oh, David. No, just a friend." Though she couldn't help but wish that maybe . . . someday.

"That's my son, Kellan, with him."

Sophie stared at the woman and noticed the tears in her eyes. "He seems to enjoy chess."

Kellan's mom nodded. "He and his father played."

"Where is his father?"

"He was killed in action in Afghanistan."

Sympathy flooded Sophie. "My condolences."

"Thanks. Greg has been gone a year and this is the first time I've seen Kellan interact with anyone without snarling. He's been so angry," she said. "Lost."

Sophie wasn't sure what to say or how to help. Her heart ached for the teenager's loss, the mother's grief.

"Sophie!" Troy hugged her leg.

"Hey, kiddo, you having fun?"

He peered up at her. "Yes. Grandma Louise said you have my costume for tonight."

"I do. And I have Riggs's costume, too."

"Pastor Jeff said we need to go get ready," Troy told her.

"Okay, let's tell your uncle." She tagged a teen girl who was standing close by to take over the refreshment table. She and Troy went to where David and the kid played just as the kid gave a triumphant "checkmate!"

David fist-bumped Kellan. "Good job."

Kellan's mother put her hand on his shoulder. "Time to go."

Kellan twisted around to stare up at his mother. "Can we stay for the service?"

Surprise widened her eyes. "Uh, sure. I'd like that." To David she said, "Thank you."

David held out his business card. "I told Kellan he can call me anytime. I'd like a rematch."

Kellan's mom took the card and nodded. With her arm around Kellan's shoulders, they walked away.

Sophie helped David put the chess pieces back. "You made the boy's day."

"He's a good kid. Hurting," David replied.

"He's hurt, too?" Troy asked. "Does he have stitches?"

Sophie caught David's gaze and they shared a smile. "No, honey," Sophie said gently. "Kellan's dad went to heaven."

"Oh, like my mommy and daddy," Troy said.

David lifted Troy into his arms. "Yes, like that. Now, shepherd boy, I think the stage is calling you."

"It is?" Troy cupped his ear with his hand. "I don't hear anything."

Sophie tweaked Troy's nose. "Silly. I'll meet you two backstage with Riggs and the costume."

She turned to leave, when David captured her hand. She lifted her gaze in question to him.

He opened his mouth to say something, then seemed to catch himself. Finally he said, "We'll see you in a bit."

❄   ❄   ❄

"For unto us, a child is born," a preteen boy's voice came through the speakers and filled the church sanctuary as he narrated the story of Christ's birth.

David sat in the front pew beside Sophie. Her grandmother and Simon sat on her other side. Sophie lifted her camera, the soft clicks of the shutter barely audible as she captured the sight before them. On the stage where the pastor normally preached, a makeshift manger scene had been erected. A doll played the part of baby Jesus, while a host of children played the various roles, acting out the story.

Riggs, wearing antlers on his massive head, lay at Troy's feet. Troy stood proud, holding his shepherd staff, dressed in a white sheet with a length of knotted rope tied about his waist. A head-dress covered his hair. On the opposite side of the stage a little girl, also dressed as a shepherd, struggled to control her goat, who nibbled at her costume. A ripple of amusement went through the audience.

Though David was proud of his nephew and pleased for him, heaviness filled David's heart, which left him feeling confused and at odds. He should be happy. Troy was doing well. He was healing from the loss of his parents as only a child could. A child who felt loved.

And oh, David loved Troy with a fierceness that at times scared him.

But it wasn't Troy who caused the oppressive weight crushing David's chest. It was the woman sitting beside him. Sophie's sweet scent filled his senses. Her goodness and light wrapped around him, making him ache for what he knew he shouldn't want.

He wanted her in his life forever.

He forced himself to concentrate on the pageant and clapped enthusiastically when it was over. Troy would be going back to the great room with the other kids during the evening sermon.

As the kids filed offstage to be replaced by the choir, restlessness filled David and he couldn't sit there any longer. He leaned in to Sophie and whispered in her ear, "I need some fresh air."

He stood and made his way outside. The night air was frigid but dry. He kept walking until he was under the branches of a large oak tree. He put his hand on the rough bark and leaned on his hand. His heart beat an erratic rhythm as a prayer lifted from his lips and swirled through the air. "Lord, I don't know what to do here. I love Sophie, but I'm too afraid to open my heart fully to her. To anyone. I couldn't bear it if something happened to her or Troy." His gut clenched. He'd lost so many people he'd loved. "Lord, please, what should I do?"

He waited, but no answer came.

* * *

Grandma nudged Sophie in the ribs with her elbow. "Where's he going?" she asked in a hushed tone.

"Needs some air," Sophie whispered back. She hoped he was okay. He'd looked a little green.

Concern shone in Grandma's eyes. "This would be a good time for you to talk to him."

A flurry of nerves rose within Sophie. This would be a perfect opportunity to tell David what was in her heart. Setting her camera back in its bag, relinquishing the equipment's care to her grandma, Sophie rose, grabbed her coat, and hurried out of the sanctuary. In the vestibule she paused to put on her coat.

The edge of the envelope that David had given her poked out of her pants pocket, snagging on the coat. She tugged it free and opened it. Her jaw tightened to see a check, along with a handwritten note. She moved closer to a wall sconce so she could read the letter.

Dear Sophie, please accept this money, not because I owe you, but because I want you to enjoy yourself on your trip. Buy something fun that makes you smile. We hope you'll come back to visit soon. We'll miss you. David.

"Ah, David," she whispered. "I'm not going anywhere."

She tucked the note back into the envelope and hurried outside. The powerful streetlamps at the front of the church provided enough illumination for her to easily find David under the massive tree in front of the church. His head was bowed.

She hesitated, afraid to intrude.

Then he straightened and spun around to face her.

His eyes widened. "Sophie? Is everything okay?"

She blew out a breath and then strode forward with purpose. "Yes, it is. I need to tell you something."

Wariness entered his gaze. "Okay."

Suddenly she felt tongue-tied as the words she wanted to say stuck in her throat.

He tilted his head. "Soph?"

"Why have you been pushing me away the past few days?" She blurted out the question, then held her breath.

He rubbed a hand over his jaw. "That's a complicated question with a complicated answer."

She dipped her chin. "Really? From where I'm standing it seems like a pretty easy question."

"Okay, the question is straightforward, but Sophie, the answer isn't." He reached out to tuck her hair behind her ears, his touch a caress. "You see, I made you a promise and I really, really want to break it."

Anticipation lifted her spirits. "What promise?"

He cupped her cheek, his thumb rubbing along her jawline. "That I wouldn't ask you to stay."

Elated by his answer, she turned her cheek into his hand. "You don't have to ask."

"What?"

She took his hands in hers and held his gaze. She needed him to know, to understand. "Grandma accused me of living my life safely behind my camera lens. She was right. My whole life I've been too scared to really live, to allow anyone too close when I was so sure no one could ever really love me."

"Sophie—"

She put a finger to his lips to stop his pained voice. "I'm ready to fully embrace life. And love. I love you, David Murphy. There is nowhere on earth I'd rather be than here with you and Troy."

For a long moment, he stood there staring at her. "Are you sure?"

"I've never been more sure of anything in my life," she told him, knowing that it was the truth. "I love you."

He tugged her closer. "I've held back my heart for so long, fearing love because it always came with pain. I've lost so many people."

She wrapped her arms around him wanting to absorb his pain. "I know. But you have me and Troy now. We're not going anywhere, God willing."

He closed his eyes for a moment. "That's it, isn't it. Only God is in control."

"Yes. We place our lives and hearts in His care."

David exhaled, the tension leaving his body. "I love you, Sophie Griffith. Enough to let you go."

Her tummy fluttered. He loved her. Excitement built in her chest.

Then the last part of his statement registered and it shook her. "But I don't want to go. Not if it means leaving you."

He gave her a crooked smile. "Then I guess Troy and I are coming with you to Zurich."

Her heart soared. Love and joy spread through her, making her limbs weak. "As much as I love that idea, no. You've a company to run and Troy has school that starts back up in a week. I will ask my agent to contact the skiwear company to see if they'd be willing to substitute the Cascades for the Alps. I'll send them a cute picture of Riggs and suggest using him in the images. And if they won't . . ." She shrugged. Nothing was more important than this man and the family they could build together. "There will be other jobs."

"No, Sophie, you need to go. I refused to allow you to give up your career for me."

"It's one job, not my career. Seattle is a thriving place with lots of opportunities for a photographer."

"You've wanted this job for a long time. It's important to your career, your dreams."

She couldn't deny that. "I'd be gone for three weeks." It would seem like a lifetime.

He cupped her cheek. "And Troy and I will be here when you return."

Her heart melted and puddled at his feet. Tears sprang to her eyes. He was such a dear, loving man. "Thank you. I love you. And come summertime, the three of us traveling together . . ." She touched his face. "I know now why my past romances failed. I wasn't ready to fully give my heart. But I am now. To you. You have my heart, David. Both you and Troy. For now and always."

He pulled her into his embrace. "I love you so much. And I need you more than I can ever tell you." He leaned back. "I have something for you." He reached into his pocket and withdrew a slim box wrapped in red glittery paper. "Until I can put a ring on your finger this will have to do."

She took the box with shaky hands and undid the wrapping. Inside lay the beautiful snowflake bracelet she'd seen in the store. "Oh, David."

He lifted the bracelet from the cotton padding and secured it around her wrist. The dangling snowflake charms sparkled in the light. Then she noticed snowflakes landing on her arm. "It's snowing for real."

He looked up and laughed when he saw that she was right.

"My mother always told me that snowflakes were kisses from angels," David murmured right before he captured her mouth for a soul-searing, heat-inducing kiss.

"Sophie, Uncle David!" Troy's exuberant cry broke them apart seconds before Troy wrapped his tiny arms around their legs. "You're kissing!"

Sophie laughed as tears of joy sprang to her eyes.

David scooped Troy into his arms. "Yes, we are."

Troy peered at them. "Does this mean we can be a family?"

"I do believe that is the plan," David said, his gaze on Sophie.

She snuggled into his side, wrapping her arm around him, the other holding Troy's hand. "Would that be okay, Troy?"

"Yay! I got what I wanted for Christmas."

Sophie shared a startled look with David. Apparently Troy had asked Santa and prayed for them to be a family. Her whole being expanded with love and gratitude.

Riggs's happy bark drew their attention to Grandma and Simon. They'd come out of the church and were standing on the walkway. Simon had his arm around Grandma and she looked quite comfortable there. Troy wiggled out of David's arms and landed on his feet at a run. He and Riggs played in the falling snow.

Sophie turned to David. "Will you accept my apology for telling Grandma about the app? I didn't think she would mention it to Simon. But obviously they're a couple. And couples—"

"Tell each other everything," he finished for her and wiped a snowflake from her nose. "I forgive you. Will you accept my apology for overreacting?"

"Yes." She peered at him with a grin. "You do that often, you know."

He shrugged with a sheepish expression crossing his handsome face. "I'm not perfect."

She laughed. "Good thing, because I'm not either."

"To me you are." He placed a quick kiss on her lips before urging her forward to join the older couple.

"What a merry Christmas this has turned out to be." Grandma beamed and laid her head on Simon's shoulder.

"Yes, indeed. A very merry Christmas," Sophie agreed, hugging David.

"Should we head home for a proper family Christmas Eve dinner?" Grandma asked. "And the presents under the tree?"

Sophie smiled up at David. "Yes, a family for Christmas. The best gift ever."

EPILOGUE

The small dressing room off the vestibule of the Good Hope Christian Church was fragrant with the aroma of a dozen gardenias and roses. Sophie lifted her camera to take a picture of the beautiful bouquets resting on a side table. She turned the camera toward the vanity, where her grandma sat while Sophie's mom fussed with Grandma's hair.

"Smile, ladies," Sophie instructed.

Both women met the camera lens with bright smiles in the mirror.

Sophie clicked off several shots. "Perfect."

Her mom looked stunning with her hair, still blond thanks to a good hairdresser, twisted into a fancy knot at the back of her head. A string of pearls rested just above the collar of her lilac-colored, designer dress suit.

Mom had curled Grandma's hair and now fastened a headdress with seed pearls to her silver hair. The blush pink silk dress, reminiscent of old Hollywood, highlighted the soft blush high on Grandma's cheeks.

A knock sounded at the door. Sophie set aside her camera and moved to open it.

"Stop!" Mom called as she hurried to block Sophie.

"If it's the groom, he can't see the bride before the ceremony," Mom stated. "I'll answer it."

Sophie held up her hands in surrender. Mom liked to be in control, though she'd hired one of LA's best wedding planners to fly up to Washington and coordinate the event.

Mom opened the door. Sophie heard David's deep voice on the other side. Her heart skipped several beats. Ever since she returned from her trip in the Alps two weeks ago, she, David, and Troy had spent every moment possible together. Troy was doing well in school and David finally finished his app and was ready to roll it out next month.

Sophie's photo shoot had been a success, and the client had already put her on hold for July, when the company would reveal a new line of active wear. She was hoping the shoot would be somewhere that David and Troy would like to visit.

Mom shut the door and leaned against it. Her cheeks were flushed and her eyes bright. "That was David. He wants to talk to you."

Sophie took a step.

"Wait." Mom gathered Sophie's hands into hers. "I like your young man. Very thoughtful. He and Troy came to LA while you were gone."

Sophie blinked in surprise. "They did?"

"Yes. They came to officially ask your father for your hand in marriage."

"He did?" A joyful thrill raced through her. That was so sweet and old-fashioned. And something her dad would have liked. Sophie swung her gaze to Grandma. "Did you know about this?"

Grandma swiveled on the vanity stool and smiled, looking pleased. "I did."

Mom squeezed Sophie's hands. "We're very proud of you, Soph."

Sophie's heart clenched. "You are?"

"Of course. You are such a beautiful, talented woman and I'm so happy you've finally found someone to share your life with." Mom's eyes misted with tears.

"Thank you, Mom." Sophie hugged her.

Disengaging and smoothing out her dress, Mom waved her hand toward the door. "David's waiting."

Sophie stepped out to find both David and Troy waiting for her. The pair looked stunningly handsome in matching tuxedos. Troy held a small pillow with two beautiful rings tied to the center. At Troy's feet lay Riggs, sporting a black bow tie. His coat had been brushed to a gleaming sheen. He rose to his feet as she approached. Her three men. Her heart expanded in her chest, nearly bursting with love.

David opened his arms and Sophie glided into his embrace.

"Is everything okay?" Sophie asked.

"Yes." David pulled back to look into her eyes. "I have something to ask you."

Troy tugged at David's jacket.

David smiled. "We have something to ask you."

"Uncle David, you know Grandma said you have to go on one knee."

Sophie's pulse kicked into high gear. One knee?

"Right." David released Sophie to go on bent knee. From the inside pocket of his jacket he produced a small black jewelry box.

Sophie's breath caught and held.

David opened the box to reveal a dazzling engagement ring. A wreath of hearts of fire diamonds surrounded a flawless center diamond, creating a truly elegant snowflake. "Sophie Griffith, I love you. Will you marry me?"

Tears of joy filled her eyes. "Yes, a thousand times yes."

David slipped the ring onto her finger. It fit perfectly. "Oh, David, I love you, too." She tugged him to his feet and pressed her lips to his.

Troy giggled and Riggs let out a happy-sounding bark, lifting Sophie's heart.

The deep sound of a throat clearing broke them apart. Her father stood behind David, tall and broad-shouldered. A silver fox looking sharp in his black tux. His blue eyes, eyes so like Grandma's, twinkled in the wall sconce lights.

"Dad." Sophie held up her hand. "Look."

Her dad grinned. "It's wonderful. I'm so happy for you both."

Sophie hugged her father. "Thank you," she whispered into his ear.

He embraced her back with gentleness, then set her free and wiped at his eyes.

"Grandma Louise," Troy said. "You look beautiful."

They all turned to see her grandma gliding forward, a vision in her wedding gown. Mom handed Sophie her bridesmaid bouquet.

"Places everyone," the diminutive wedding coordinator from LA commanded with a clap of her hands. She had a headset on and spoke into it. "Start the processional music."

David held out his arm to Mom and led her inside the sanctuary.

"Okay, ring bearer and, uh, companion, you're up," the wedding planner said, urging Troy and Riggs to walk down the aisle.

Panic flashed across Troy's face. Sophie put her hand on his shoulder. "I'll be right behind you two."

He nodded and moved forward. Riggs walked beside him, his large paws padding softly on the red carpet runner. Sophie followed close behind the pair as her father offered Grandma his arm.

The sanctuary was filled with family and friends. At the altar, Simon Bichon stood with a tender smile on his handsome face. Beside him stood his son, who'd flown in from back east, and David.

Sophie took her place and met David's loving gaze. One day soon it would be Sophie's turn to commit her life and love to the man of her dreams. She couldn't be more blessed.

ACKNOWLEDGMENTS

I would like to express my heartfelt gratitude to several people who made this book possible. Thank you to Jessica Alvarez for the years of encouragement and support, as first my editor and now as my agent. I appreciate your believing in me. Thank you to Beth Adams and everyone at Howard Books for taking a chance on a new-to-you author. It's been a pleasure working on this book with you. Thank you to my family for always being supportive during the deadline days. And finally, thank you to author Leah Vale—I couldn't ask for a better friend and critique partner.